SWEET TEA & HONEY BEES

RACHEL HANNA

CHAPTER 1

*K*ate's blood pressure had to be high. She felt her face flushing as her hand gripped the back of the barstool, her fingers turning white. "Brandon, I'm going to say this one more time so that maybe, just maybe, you'll actually listen. Your daughter doesn't want to talk to you right now. This is her decision. If you keep texting her and calling her, you're going to ruin any chance to have a relationship with her. Don't you understand that?"

"You can't keep her from me, Kate. Not only is it not right, but I can take you to court. You know that, don't you?"

She took in a deep breath and blew it out through pursed lips just like her yoga teacher had taught her. Zoe, her instructor and the cutest yogi she'd ever seen, had explained that blowing through pursed lips and extending her exhales would relieve stress. Kate also believed that seeing Brandon in

RACHEL HANNA

person and putting her hands around his neck could achieve stress relief as well.

"You need to stop threatening me with court, Brandon. Your daughter is almost sixteen years old, and no judge is going to force her to spend time with a father who abandoned her years ago. It's been weeks since you texted her, and she still doesn't want contact. Why can't you respect her wishes?"

"Because I know you're influencing her."

Kate let go of the chair and sat down, rubbing her temple with her other hand. "That's not true. I've told her over and over that I'm okay if she wants to have a relationship with you."

"And she knows you don't mean that. I'm sure you've dragged my name through the mud so much that she thinks I'm the devil."

"Brandon, your actions have done a fine job of that without me saying a thing."

"I wanted to spend Christmas with her this year, and now that opportunity has passed." She looked over at the Christmas tree that was still standing in the corner of the living room, calling for her to take it down now that January had rolled around.

"Seriously? You thought your daughter, who you haven't contacted in years, would want to come spend Christmas with you? Have you experienced a recent head injury? Or are you taking a new medication?"

"Funny. Look, here's all I'm going to say. I will be involved in my daughter's life, one way or another. I need you to talk to her."

"I've already talked to her, and I've certainly talked to you as much as I'm going to. Goodbye, Brandon."

As she pressed end, she heard him start to argue, but thankfully his voice disappeared with the press of a button. Kate growled loudly, thankful that the B&B was currently empty of guests, and slid her phone across the counter. It bounced off the retro chrome toaster and ran right into the side of the refrigerator. The screen protector, a valuable purchase, cracked in two spots.

"Yikes! What was that about?" Mia walked through the French doors from the backyard, a Christmas wreath on one arm and a blow mold snowman in her other hand.

"That man is infuriating." Kate walked across the kitchen and picked up her phone, inspecting it to make sure the screen protector had done its job.

"Brandon?"

"Yep. I don't know why he can't understand that Evie has made the decision to not have contact with him."

"Is he still threatening legal action?"

Kate sighed. "Yes. I just don't get his angle. He's supposedly happily married to Kara," she said, saying his wife's name like it was a curse word.

Mia rubbed her shoulder. "I know this must be hard. I wish I had some advice for you, but having never been married and never having a kid, I don't think my advice would be helpful."

Kate looked at her. "If you have advice, I'd still love to hear it."

Mia leaned against the counter. "Look, Momma always told me that fear of the unknown was usually worse than reality. Maybe you just need to invite Brandon here and deal with whatever he's up to."

"But, Evie doesn't want contact with him."

"Are you sure about that?" Mia cocked her head to the side and scrunched her nose.

"What do you know that I don't know?"

"I promised Evie I'd keep her confidence, but in this case I think that might be doing more harm than good. So, I'm making an executive decision."

"What are you talking about?"

"Evie is somewhat interested in seeing her dad."

"But, she's told me the exact opposite!"

Mia smiled sadly. "I know, hon, but she's just afraid that it would be too much for you, seeing Brandon and all. She doesn't want to hurt you."

Kate sat down in one of the bar stools and put her head in her hands. This parenting thing was rough stuff. Just when she thought she was getting the hang of it, something new happened to show her just how behind the eight ball she was.

"I don't want to see that man," she admitted. Maybe she had been giving off that energy to Evie. Maybe Brandon was actually right about that. The thought of him being right about anything made her cringe.

"I know you don't." Mia sat down beside her, a look of empathy on her face. Kate felt safe with her sister, like she could say or do anything and still be loved and accepted. Finding her sister had been one of the greatest gifts of her life, and she often wondered if this is what it would've felt like to know her mother. After all, Mia was the closest she would ever get to meeting the woman who had given her life. "But, maybe this will give you the closure you need."

"I'm afraid I'm just opening Pandora's box by letting him into Evie's life."

"Look, Evie is almost an adult. She's going to start making her own decisions in a couple of years. Personally, I think a lot of her acting out has been about feeling abandoned by her dad. Maybe this will heal something in her."

Kate knew she was right. Keeping Evie away from her father might have been more detrimental than just ripping off the bandage and letting the chips fall where they may.

"I'll talk to her," Kate said, knowing that she couldn't keep having the same conversation with Brandon over and over.

"Good. I know it's hard, sis. If you need me, you know I'm here, right?"

Kate smiled as she laid her head on Mia's shoulder. "Ditto."

TRAVIS STARED out over the ridge, his camera suspended in mid-air, waiting for the perfect shot.

Sunsets were his favorite, when the blue sky disappeared and was replaced by the most amazing oranges, yellows and pinks. Against the backdrop of the Blue Ridge Mountains, there was nothing quite as beautiful… except for Mia, of course.

Since coming home to Carter's Hollow and reconnecting with Mia again, he'd never felt so much joy. His heart literally felt like it might explode at times, and his cheeks often hurt from smiling. Just being near her gave him a sense of calm and serenity that had been missing for so many years.

They were promising to take it slow, but there were times he wanted to just drop to one knee and pop the question. It felt as if he needed to nail things down and make them official before some other man realized what a goddess he got to call his girlfriend.

For the last few months, they'd spent so much time together, hiking the trails around the B&B, preparing peach cobbler for the guests and having big family dinners on Sundays. It was like a big family, and he loved it. By some miracle, he and Cooper had become actual friends, often taking one day a week to go fishing or repair something around the B&B.

Still, he had a longing. An urge. A need to take his career further. When he'd left Carter's Hollow all those years ago, he'd planned to do great things with his photography. But, he'd spent years taking pictures of hamburgers and French fries for fast food companies instead. There was just nothing overly artistic about making sure a pickle was properly placed for a photo.

As the sun finally dropped below the mountain ridge, he held up his camera and snapped the first shot. The pinks in the sky tonight were hard to describe. Any time someone told him they didn't believe in God, he wondered if they'd ever seen a sunset over blue tinged mountains. Like a painting straight from God himself, it was sure to change anyone's mind about there not being a Creator.

"Sorry I'm late," Mia said from behind. "I brought coffee. Man, it's chilly up here!"

January in Carter's Hollow was still frigid. They'd had one snow so far that season, but more were sure to come. Especially in the higher elevations, snow was common during the winter months and even into early spring.

"Thanks, babe," Travis said, looking up at her. He was sitting on his favorite outcropping of rocks, his legs dangling over the edge. Mia handed him the coffee, put a blanket down beside him and gingerly sat down, using his shoulder for stability.

"I don't know why you like sitting right at the edge. It still scares me to death," she said, shaking a bit from the air.

"You know I'd never let anything happen to you," he said, giving her a quick peck on the lips. He took a long sip of the coffee, which was just the right temperature after Mia's walk to find him.

"Get any good pictures?"

He looked back out toward the sunset and realized

he'd missed the shot he was going for, but he wasn't about to make Mia feel bad. He would gladly miss all of his shots for a chance to spend time with her.

"A few. Here, check them out," he said, handing her the camera. She set her coffee beside her and scrolled through the pictures on his digital display.

"This one is beautiful. Looks like a painting. I love all the pink."

He took the camera back from her. "Yeah, that's my favorite. I'm thinking about having it blown up so I can hang it over my couch."

"That would be beautiful." She took another sip of her coffee and stared off into the distance. "Kate heard from Brandon again."

"Ugh. I feel like I need to find that guy and have a private conversation with him. I'm sure Cooper would be on board."

Mia chucked. "I'm sure Cooper would love nothing more. He and Kate are getting pretty serious, and I don't think he likes this whole thing with Brandon."

Travis bumped her shoulder. "Are we getting serious?"

She shrugged her shoulders and smiled that crooked smile of hers. "I don't know. Are we?"

Before he could respond, his phone buzzed in his pocket. "Hold that thought," he said, holding up his finger. "Hello?"

"Travis?"

"Yeah?"

"It's Sam Lively!"

His mouth dropped open. "Sam? Wow! I haven't talked to you in ages. What's going on?"

"You're a hard man to find! Listen, I've got a business proposition for you. I was wondering if we could meet for a chat? I'll be flying into Atlanta next week, so I thought I could rent a car and come to you?"

"Sure! I'd love to see you!"

"Great. I'll call you when I land."

"Sounds good. See you soon." He ended the call and put his phone back in his pocket.

"Who's Sam?" Mia asked.

"I worked with Sam back in New York. We were on the same ad campaigns a few times."

"What did Sam want?"

"There's some business proposition we need to discuss next week."

"Oh, that sounds promising. Nothing that will take you away from me for too long, I hope?"

Travis put his arm around her as she put her head on his shoulder. "Absolutely nothing will ever take me away from you again, Mia. You can count on that."

～

"THANKS FOR HELPING WITH DINNER," Kate said to her daughter. Evie had been learning the ropes at the B&B with the hopes that one day she might run it.

The land seemed to already be in her blood, a fact that delighted Mia to no end.

"No problem. I'm getting the hang of that country fried steak. Even Aunt Mia said so. She said grandma would've been really proud of me."

Kate touched her cheek. "I'm sure she would. And I'm really proud of you too, sweetie. You've done so well since we moved here. Well, except for a couple of hiccups here and there."

Evie chuckled. "I'm a teenager, Mom. What do you expect?" She wiped down the kitchen table and put the placemats back into place. Mia had recently changed them out from the Christmas decor to a basic blue and white pattern to match her mother's antique dishes. Soon, she'd be ready to decorate for spring.

Kate walked over and sat down at the table, patting the seat across from her. "Have a seat. We need to chat."

Evie stared at her for a moment. "Whatever it is, I didn't do it."

"You didn't do anything wrong. That I know of, anyway."

"Thanks for the vote of confidence," she said, rolling her eyes as she tossed the rag onto the table.

"Listen, your father called again today."

Evie groaned. "What do you want me to do, Mom? I can't make him stop calling you. I don't answer his texts or calls. Maybe we should change our numbers."

Kate reached over and grabbed her hand. "I know you want to see him, Ev."

"What? No, I don't. I already told you that, like, a million times."

"You don't have to try to save my feelings. If you want to see your father, I won't stand in your way."

Evie sighed. "It's fine, Mom. I don't need him in my life. He just walked out and built a new family. I don't know what he wants with me anyway."

"Maybe you need to talk to him and ask."

Evie stood up and put her hands on her hips. "Why are you saying this all of the sudden?"

Kate bit both of her lips, a habit she'd had since childhood. "Your Aunt Mia was concerned…"

"I'm going to smack her when I see her…" Evie said under her breath.

"She loves you. And I love you. And if what you want is to see your father and have some kind of relationship, I will fully support you."

Evie sat back down. "I don't know what I want."

Kate reached behind her and picked up Evie's phone that was charging at the end of the breakfast bar. "Here. Start with responding to a text. See what he says. I'm here no matter what."

Evie stared at her for a long moment and then looked down at her phone. "I'll think about it. Can I go do my homework now?"

"Of course."

As she watched Evie walk up the stairs, it hurt her heart to think of how she must have been struggling with the decision before her. A father should love his daughter so much that there is never a question. No daughter should have to think so hard about texting her own father. It wasn't fair, and she wasn't sure how she'd react if she saw Brandon again.

Her new relationship with her own father had been such a godsend, and it pained her to think that Evie may never have that. That she might choose the wrong man one day looking for love because her own father hadn't provided what she needed emotionally.

Sometimes, life just wasn't fair.

JACK STARED AT SYLVIA, his face hot with anger. "I said no."

"But, Jack, they should know…"

"Sylvia, stop. You're making everything worse. Can't you just let me make my own decisions. For once?"

She rolled her eyes. "Really? You make all of your own decisions, and rarely the right ones!"

As she stormed down the hallway of their home and slammed the bedroom room, Jack stood there, his suitcase in his hand and wondered what to do. The right answer was eluding him tonight, so he walked out the front door and climbed into his truck, heading off down the highway towards Sweet Tea B&B.

CHAPTER 2

*K*ate walked out onto the back deck, the morning air still quite cold. She couldn't wait for spring. The beautiful weather, the gorgeous flowers and her new beekeeping and honey business would hopefully be flourishing. One thing was for sure, she never thought she'd be learning so much about bees.

"Good morning, hot stuff," Cooper said from around the corner. He was often hanging around the backyard these days, working on her beekeeping area and a new greenhouse that Mia had requested. Thankfully, they had plenty of land to work with.

"Hot stuff? I like it," she said. He leaned down and kissed her head.

"When are the bees coming in?"

"Hopefully, next week. I ordered nucleus colonies so I'll get the bees and the whole box setup."

"Good. We'll be ready."

"Also, I already ordered the labels for the honey."

He smiled. "Planning for success, I see?"

"Is there any other way? This has to be a success. This B&B can't make more money than it's making without a new revenue stream. And I have to send Evie to college at some point."

"Did she text her dad?"

Kate sighed. "Honestly, I don't know. She left for school early this morning, and I didn't want to press her."

"How are you feeling about it?"

"Like I want to order murderous hornets to attack him when he arrives. Is that too dark?"

Cooper laughed and sat down next to her. "Maybe just a tad."

"Well, it's how I feel today. Maybe tomorrow will be better."

"Any new guests arriving today?"

"We had a check-out this morning, and I think we have a new guest this afternoon. I didn't even look at the name, but I managed to get room three set up."

He reached for her hand and squeezed it. "You know this whole thing with Evie will work out, right?"

She sighed. "I hope so. As much as it has pained me over the years to see her struggle without a father figure, if I'm honest, it was easier for me. Brandon wrecked our lives, and I never wanted to see or hear from him again. I guess that was selfish on my part. Maybe I should've tried harder to make him have a relationship with her."

"I'm not a dad yet, but I don't think that's how it works, Kate. He should've wanted to be with her. He should've needed his daughter in his life. A dad doesn't have to be forced to be with his kid. There's something wrong with him, not you."

She smiled at him. "You're very sweet."

He stood up and shrugged his shoulders. "I'm sweet like 'Sweet Charlene's Honey,'" he said, pretending to do a commercial.

"Get back to work!" Kate said as she stood up and headed back into the house.

"Hey, Kate?"

"Yeah," she said, turning back to him.

"You're not alone in this. You know that, right?"

She nodded. "I know. And thank you."

As she walked back into the house, she felt grateful for Cooper's support. And for Mia's. But, in the end, the showdown would be between her and Brandon. She knew him well enough to know that he was up to something, and he had an ulterior motive. To protect her daughter, she had to figure out what it was.

MIA SAT in the rocking chair on the front porch and stared out over the lake. It was very still today, like a mirror reflecting the mountains surrounding it. Off in the distance, she could hear a hawk squawking at something. She pulled the wool blanket around her tightly and held a cup of coffee in her hands, trying to keep them warm.

As cold as it was this morning, she wanted to be outside. She loved being out there, watching nature in full force, hearing all of the sounds that went with it.

Kate had gone upstairs to work on the accounting numbers, something Mia hated to do. She decided to take a moment before the new guest arrived to just enjoy some time alone. Plus, she was trying not to think about the fact that Travis was currently meeting his friend, Sam, about some business opportunity.

She wanted him to pursue his dreams, of course. But, the last time he'd pursued those dreams, she'd gotten left behind. Having that happen all over again would be devastating, as much as she hated to admit it. She liked to think of herself as an independent woman who didn't need a man, but she felt like she needed Travis as much as the air she breathed. It was uncomfortable to care about someone that much, and it often felt too vulnerable.

He'd promised her he would never leave again, not without her, at least. But could she keep him from pursuing some big dream? What if he was getting a job offer in New York again? Or Paris? Could she stop him and live with herself?

For her part, she never planned to leave Sweet Tea B&B. It was her home and in her blood. Now that Kate and Evie were there too, it felt more final. It was their heritage, and that was something her mother would've loved. She felt her momma's presence every single day at the B&B. She was in the smell of the lavender potpourri in the guest baths. She was in the softness of the blanket thrown over the arm chair by the fireplace. She was in the thick oak wood that made up the bannister that she gripped as she walked down the stairs during those last few months of her cancer battle.

She *was* Sweet Tea B&B.

There were days when she woke up crying because she'd dreamed about her. There were nights she went to sleep crying because she needed her. Grief was a funny thing. It meant you loved someone, but it brought some of the worst pain a person could experience. Love meant grieving one day, and that was a difficult trade-off to make.

She felt her eyes swell with tears, but the moment was broken by tires moving down the gravel driveway. Deciding it must be her new guest, she wiped away the stray tears, took a deep breath and stood up to greet the new arrival. Then, she realized that she recognized the truck. It was her father.

Jack parked and jumped out, stretching his tall, lanky limbs a bit before walking over to the porch with a smile on his face. "Hey there!"

"Dad? What're you doing here?" She loved saying 'Dad'. It was something she never thought she'd do, but Jack had made it so easy.

"Thought I'd come surprise my girls for a few days. That okay?"

She walked down the steps, slinging her much-needed blanket over the railing, and hugged him. He was so tall, she had to get on her tip-toes and he had to lean down just so they could embrace.

"Where's Sylvia?"

He cleared his throat. "Oh, well, she's busy at the moment. Working on some stuff for the volunteering she does. Besides, I needed some time alone with you girls."

"So, you're the new guest?"

"Yeah. Sorry, I made up a name. I just wanted to surprise y'all."

She laughed. "You're always welcome, Dad. You know that. Come on in!"

He grabbed his bag from the back of his truck and followed her up the stairs. Mia retrieved her blanket. She turned back to him.

"Are you sure things are okay with you and Sylvia?"

He smiled. "Of course, darlin'. Everything is just fine."

For some reason, she didn't believe a word he was saying right now.

KATE STOOD IN THE KITCHEN, stirring the massive amounts of sugar into the warm tea. Mia had shown her how to make it "the right way" so many times. First, she had to put hot water in the plastic pitcher with several large tea bags. Then, she had to set it in the window so that it got plenty of sun for a couple of hours. Finally, she poured tons of sugar into it, stirred and then topped it off with cold water.

Sweet tea was the name of the B&B, but she still hadn't developed a taste for it yet. It didn't gag her as much now, but being from up north, she'd never drank the thick, sugary beverage until recently. Mia assured her that she'd be a regular sweet tea drinker in no time.

"I still can't believe you're here, Dad."

Jack smiled as he sat at the breakfast bar watching his daughter. "I just needed a visit with my girls. Is that so wrong?"

"Of course not, but I just hope things are okay with you and Sylvia. She's a lovely woman."

"She sure is," he said, taking a sip of his coffee. "You girls never need to worry about me. I'm the father. I do the worrying."

Kate laughed. "I wish that was how it worked, but I do my fair share of worrying."

"Mia told me about your ex-husband. What's his name? Brandon?"

"Yep," Kate said, holding the pitcher under the water filter. "And he's a louse."

"Need me to have a word with him?"

Kate thought he was joking, but Jack had a look on his face she hadn't seen before. A protective, fatherly look. It gave her a warm feeling inside.

"No. But, thank you."

"Don't let him push you around. If you don't think Evie should have a relationship with him…"

Kate stopped him. "I do think she should try."

"Really?"

She shrugged her shoulders. "Well, I'm trying. Brandon was an awesome dad when Evie was younger. But, when we divorced and he took off with Kara, it's like he just left her behind without a thought. I never would've imagined it."

"I hope he doesn't hurt her like that again. I can't promise what I might do," Jack said, his jaw tightening. "I mean, I just met my granddaughter recently, but I love her, and no one is going to mistreat her."

Kate struggled not to burst into tears. She wasn't sad. She was thankful to finally have a real father. A dad. "Thank you."

"For what?" he asked, reaching over and touching her hand.

"For finally being here and for stepping up to be my Dad. And Mia's. And Evie's grandfather."

"I would've stepped up long ago…"

"I know. It's all in the past. I'm just glad you're here now, Dad."

"Me too, Katie." He sometimes called her Katie instead of Kate, and she loved it. It made her feel like a little girl again.

"School sucks!" Evie called as she walked in the front door. She flung her backpack onto the sofa and groaned.

"Well, welcome home to you too, kiddo," Jack said with a laugh.

"Grandpa? You're here! I didn't know you were coming!" She ran into his arms and gave him a big hug.

"It was a spur of the moment thing."

Evie looked around. "Where's Grandma Sylvia?"

"She's at home. Just took a quick solo trip to see you girls."

"Oh. Okay. Good. Maybe we can fish after dinner?"

"Of course. I never say no to fishing."

"So, what was so terrible about school?" Kate asked.

Evie walked to the refrigerator and took out a cold bottle of Coca-Cola. Mia loved getting the old-time glass bottles when she could find them.

"Well, Mrs. Gennison gave us a pop quiz in history, which I didn't do well on…"

"You didn't study?" Kate asked.

Evie stared at her. "It was a *pop* quiz. You can't study for something you don't know is coming."

"Go on…"

"Then, I had a science project I forgot was due today so I get ten points off even if I turn it on Monday. Oh, and then Lyra Kameron told the whole PE class that I couldn't climb the rope, so I did to prove that I could. And look what I did to my leg." She pulled up her shorts and revealed a burn on her inner thigh.

"Evie! Good Lord! Did you go to the school nurse and get any ointment for that?"

She laughed. "The school nurse is a joke. I swear the woman is as old as these mountains and all she has are cheap bandages and a thermometer."

"Come upstairs so I can put something on that," Kate said, walking toward the stairs.

Evie groaned as she followed her mother. "I'll be down later, Grandpa. Get that fishing pole ready!"

MIA KNEADED THE DOUGH, preparing the biscuits for dinner. They had two new guests at the B&B, but both of them were there for a relaxing getaway, so she hadn't seen much of them yet.

There was a man, Dennis, who was just traveling through on his way to Tennessee to see his family. He said he needed a couple of quiet days fishing on the lake before he had to deal with his crazy relatives.

Then there was a young woman, Tabitha, who was there for some quiet time away from her husband and three young children. The kids, all under five years old, were apparently driving her crazy.

Mia often wondered how that felt to have a husband and kids. She hoped to know what it felt like one day, but she didn't want to rush things with Travis. Having just reconnected, they both preferred to take things slow. But, sometimes she heard her biological clock ticking so loud that she couldn't sleep at night.

She wanted to be a mom. She wanted to rock a baby, make bottles, change diapers. She wanted to be the room mom in her child's classroom. She wanted to make school lunches and put little notes in them like her mother did. She wanted to cut sandwiches into the little shapes, help with homework and go trick-or-treating again.

When she thought too hard about it, her heart started to ache. And it was a weird ache because she was missing a person who didn't exist. Or maybe they did exist out there in the world beyond this one, waiting for their soul to be put into just the right body. Her mother used to tell her not to rush so much. She said that the perfect things would come into her life at the most perfect moments because that's how God worked. But, lately, there were times she was afraid that God had forgotten her.

Of course, she was more than grateful for the blessings in her life like her new sister, niece and father. She was blessed beyond measure to have Travis back too. But she wanted to be a mother, and there was just no getting around that.

"Need any help?" Travis asked as he walked through the front door. She loved seeing him at the end of the day. It felt like they were married, so comfortable with each other from years of knowing one another.

"Nope. Just about to put these biscuits in the oven and then wait for the chicken to finish cooking."

He walked into the kitchen and put his arms around her waist as she was cutting the biscuits with the old tin can her mother had used. "Somebody is in a good mood?"

"I'm just happy to see you is all," he said, pressing a kiss to her neck.

She turned around and faced him, kissing the edge of his jaw where the stubble had grown over the last few hours. "Staying for dinner?"

"Actually, no. Sam got to town early, so I was going to meet up to discuss that project..."

She crinkled her nose. "No dinner with you tonight?" They had developed a tradition, of sorts, by always having dinner together each night no matter how busy the day had been.

"Are you going to be mad at me?"

She laughed. "Of course not! I want you to be happy, and if this project turns out to be something to make you happy, then I'm all for it."

"Thank you. It means a lot that you want me to do what I love." He pulled her into a tight hug.

"As long as you never leave me again," she added softly. He grunted and pulled her closer, as she wondered what this project might change about their relationship. For some reason, she had a really funny feeling about it.

"Mom?" Evie said from the door of the office. Kate had worked for hours after dinner, adding numbers to the accounting software and working on her business plan for Sweet Charlene's Honey.

"I thought you were already asleep," Kate said.

Evie shook her head. "I couldn't sleep. Can we talk?"

"Of course. Sit down."

Evie sat across from her mother, holding her favorite stuffed animal she'd had since she was three years old. Tattered and dirty, the plush teddy bear had seen better days. But, Evie refused to give it up and still slept with it every single night. Kate often wondered if she'd still sleep with it when she got married one day.

"I want to talk about… Dad."

Kate had known this conversation was coming. She'd tried to stay out of it unless Evie brought it up, and now was apparently the time.

"Okay. What's going on?"

"We've been talking a little, just on text."

"Good. I'm glad you're reconnecting with your father, Evie."

"Really? Or are you just saying that?"

Kate sighed. "I really am. A girl should have her father. I know that better than anyone."

Evie looked rattled, almost scared. "He says he's sorry."

"He should feel sorry." She said it before she could stop herself and then instantly regretted her words. Kate had long believed that kids should never be in the middle of parents. They shouldn't carry those burdens.

"Mom…"

"Sorry."

"Anyway, he um…"

"What, Evie?"

"He wants to come visit."

Kate struggled to breathe. "Here? He wants to come here?"

Evie looked at her for a long moment. "I live here, Mom. Where else is he supposed to see me?"

In that moment, she realized she would be seeing Brandon again. It hadn't really dawned on her that he'd come there, although she didn't know why. She would never send her daughter to stay with him after so many years apart. The safest situation was for him to come to the B&B, as much as she hated the thought.

"When?"

"Next weekend."

"Wow. That soon. Okay… I'll have to check the schedule."

"I… um… well, I already asked Aunt Mia to look."

"What? Why?"

"Because I wasn't sure if you'd tell the truth about whether we were booked or not."

Kate was in shock. "You thought I would lie to you?"

"Not lie… just maybe make it seem like Dad couldn't stay here…"

"Evie, I'm your mother. I love you. I would never lie to you, and I thought you knew that."

"I just thought you wouldn't want him to stay here… at the B&B."

Kate leaned back in her chair and rubbed the

bridge of her nose before looking back at her daughter. "To be honest, it's not something I'm looking forward to, having your father in the same house. But, I know you need this, and I want you to have what you need. I want this to be a good experience for you. So, I will do whatever it takes to make this work. For you. Not for him."

Evie smiled slightly. "Thanks, Mom. I'm kinda scared about it, but I think I just need to see him."

"Then I'm happy for you. I really hope it goes well."

Evie stood up and walked toward the door. "Goodnight."

"Hey, Evie?"

"Yeah?"

"You know I'm always here for you, right? No matter what?"

She nodded and smiled. "I know, Mom."

CHAPTER 3

*M*ia sat nervously at the cafe in town, tapping her fingernail against the side of her white coffee cup. She loved the thick, old restaurant ware cups that reminded her of retro diners. She imagined there used to be a jukebox in this place, once upon a time. Gone were the checker-board floors and chrome fixtures, instead replaced by a trendier faux wood floor and less harsh lighting.

She loved old stuff, often spending her spare time scouring through antique stores and looking for estate sales. Garage sale season was her favorite and was something she and her mother did together a lot. There were so many parts of Charlene that she missed, and sometimes the memories crept up on her when she least expected it.

"Sorry I'm late," Travis said, kissing the top of her head before sitting down. He grabbed the menu and started looking at it, his breath quick.

"Are you okay?"

"Yeah. Sorry. It's been a busy day. Sam and I took a quick hike so I could point out some areas of interest for the project. Then I had a video conference call about the project too. I can't wait to tell you all about it."

"And when will that be? I've barely seen you for two days."

He looked at her, an apology already written on his handsome face. "I'm really sorry, Mia. It's just that this opportunity has a deadline, and we're trying to throw things together as quickly as possible."

"Can you tell me about..."

"Hi, darlin'. What can I get you to drink?" Carla, their normal server at the cafe, stood there with a smile on her face, waiting for Travis's order since Mia had already placed hers.

"Hey, Carla. I'll take a turkey sandwich, hold the onions. And some potato salad and a sweet tea. Thanks." He handed her the menu and turned his attention back to Mia. "So, what were you saying again?"

"I wanted to know when you were going to tell me about this opportunity, as you keep calling it?"

"Well, I asked Sam to meet us here, if that's okay. Figured it'd be better coming from the horse's mouth, so to speak."

"Okay..."

Travis turned his head and looked through the

large window overlooking the town square. It was a school day, which meant the streets were fairly empty, save for the occasional person walking to and from the small office complex down the street.

"There's Sam now. Let me wave at her," he said, holding his arm in the air.

Her? When did Sam become a *her?* How hadn't it dawned on Mia that Sam might be a female?

It wasn't like it was a big deal for Sam to be a female. Women were just as successful as men in the business world, especially in the big city. No big deal…

Until Mia looked up and saw Sam in all her glory.

Goddess didn't begin to describe how she looked. Tall, leggy, blond. Busty. Perfect skin, toned legs, a toothy white smile that belonged on a dental billboard or a toothpaste commercial. And she was smiling at Travis. She hadn't noticed homely, short little Mia sitting at the table.

"I almost walked past this cute little place," she said, in a very loud, very northern voice. She thought Kate had an accent, but this lady stuck out like a sore thumb around here.

Travis gave her a quick hug. "Sam, I want you to meet Mia."

Sam smiled her broad toothy grin - seriously how did she get that many teeth in her mouth - and reached out her perfectly manicured hand. Mia forced a smile and shook her hand.

"Nice to meet you, Mia. I've heard a lot about you."

"Nice to meet you too," Mia said, wanting to follow it up with *"Really, because he didn't tell me a whole lot about you."*

"Here, have a seat. Do you want to order something?" Travis asked.

"No, thank you. I'm still stuffed from breakfast. I had a huge green smoothie at the hotel."

"I can't believe that held you over on our hike," Travis said with a chuckle.

"Hotel? Where are you staying?" Mia asked, trying to make small talk.

"In Atlanta. I just felt more comfortable there. But, Travis told me you have an adorable B&B?"

"Yes. I owned it with my mother, but she passed away recently, so now my sister runs it with me."

"So sorry to hear about your mother. Your B&B is called Sweet Pea, right?"

"Sweet *Tea*, actually," Mia said, trying not to grind her teeth to powder.

"Adorable," she repeated.

Mia couldn't remember a time where she felt more invisible than right now. And it was nothing that Travis or Sam was doing. She just suddenly felt inferior to this beautiful woman who was sitting there. Had Travis noticed how drop dead gorgeous she was?

"So, is anyone going to tell me about this big project?"

"Well, it's really quite extraodinary…" Sam started to say when Carla appeared at the table again.

"Can I get you anything?"

"Oh, I would love a cup of hot green tea."

Carla stared at her for a moment. "We don't have green tea. We do have sweet tea, if you'd like that?"

Sam looked like she'd landed in a country where she didn't speak the language. "No thanks. Just water with lemon, please."

Carla walked away, looking back once before disappearing into the kitchen.

"Okay, so where were we? Oh, yes, you wanted to know about the project," Sam said, smiling over at Travis. "Well, I work for a large publishing house in NYC and they want to publish a travel book for this area."

"Really? Why?"

"It's just a series of quaint travel books with real photos of special areas and possible tourist attractions."

Mia laughed. "Carter's Hollow has few tourist attractions."

Travis looked at her, a bit of a glare on his face. "There's a lot of beauty around here, Mia."

"Of course. Sorry."

She didn't know why she felt so anxious about this whole thing. Travis had already told her he was never leaving again, but she had this very peculiar feeling in the pit of her stomach.

"It truly is a beautiful area, and our company

would like for Travis to be the point person on a book about this region. Basically, he would spend a lot of time taking photos, scouting different spots that would be showcased in the book."

"Wow, Travis, that's a wonderful opportunity. It's exactly what you've always wanted to do," Mia said, reaching across the table and squeezing his hand.

"It really is. If this goes well, there could even be other areas that they could use me on."

"Oh. You mean like you would travel around the country?" Mia asked, trying not to appear bothered.

Sam smiled. "Not only the country. If he does well, he might have jobs all over the world." She grinned from ear to ear like this was some kind of wonderful news.

"Let's not get ahead of ourselves," Travis said, his voice shaking a bit. "One book at a time, right?"

"Of course. But don't worry, Mia, I'm sure you could travel with him. What an adventure that would be!"

Adventure? Mia had no desire to go traveling around the world. She was a homebody, through and through. Maybe Travis had the need to travel, but she didn't. Everything she loved was right here in Carter's Hollow.

"I just know how hard Travis has worked at his craft and how much he has always wanted to have it showcased. I'm glad I can help in some small way," Sam said. There was a familiarity between them that made Mia feel uncomfortable, and the very fact that she felt that way also made her feel bad about herself. She needed to trust him and their relationship, but the fear of losing him all over again had her feeling like a cornered animal.

"Right now, I think we just need to focus on this book. Sam and I have been scouting areas, and I think we have finalized most of what would need to be in the book. Of course, they want pictures from all four seasons, so I will be working on this for a while."

"And, what about you, Sam? Will you be sticking around while Travis takes pictures for the next few months?"

She shook her head, and waved her hand in the air as if that was the craziest thought anyone had ever come up with. "No, I have plenty to keep me busy back in the city. But I will be checking in on video chat at least once a week. And of course, Travis will need to come with me to meet with my bosses."

"Come with you? To New York?"

"That's something I wanted to talk to you about, actually. Sam said it would be better if I flew back with her for a few days just to meet with some of the higher ups. They like to put a face with the name."

"Oh. And that's not something you could do on a video chat?"

"I suppose we could, but really to solidify the deal, I think they're going to want to meet with Travis in person. I hope that's not an issue?"

Mia shook her head. "Of course not. Travis is free to do whatever he needs to do."

He looked at her, questioningly. "Are you not okay with this, Mia?"

"Why would you think that?" she said, trying to hide the concern that was brewing in her stomach. Concern over him traveling with such a beautiful woman. Concern over him traveling all over the world to take pictures for the books. Concerned that she was holding him back from his big dreams. Yep, there was plenty of concern to go around.

"I just thought I picked up on something," Travis said, quietly.

"Well, when Carla comes back with my water, I think this deserves a toast," Sam said, smiling, her teeth blinding Mia in the process. Or maybe she was being a bit dramatic.

As they waited to make the toast, Mia sat there, occasionally looking across the table at Travis, and wondering if their new start would be over before it really began.

EVIE CLIMBED high up into her favorite tree and stared out over the mountain range in the distance. She loved sitting up here, especially in the evening hours when the sun was starting to set. And today, she really needed the time to think. Her father was coming tomorrow, and she didn't know how to feel about the whole thing.

On the one hand, she wanted a father figure in her life. She wanted someone she could count on, and her father had been that for her once upon a time. But, in recent years, he'd left her behind in favor of building a whole new family, and that had hurt Evie more than she could even admit to herself.

What would it be like to see him again?

She'd had dreams over the years about seeing her dad, running into his arms and him swinging her around like he did when she was little. She dreamed of him taking her to a father-daughter dance or showing her off to his friends and telling them how proud he was of her. So many dreams - or maybe they were wishes - and none of them had come true.

Getting his text a few months ago had been shocking, and she still didn't really understand why he reached out again after all these years. Maybe he just wanted to see her. Maybe he wanted to invite her to meet her siblings. Maybe he realized what he'd done was wrong and he wanted to make everything right again.

She knew that him coming to the B&B was going to be hard for her mother. How couldn't it be?

"Am I interrupting?" Cooper asked from below.

"Oh, hey, Coop. I didn't know you were here today," she said. She really liked Cooper. He was good to her mother, and that was important. But, he'd also rescued her from trouble a couple of times already. She felt safer with him around.

"Mind if I come up?"

"Sure, come on up!"

The tree limbs on the large oak tree were plenty

strong enough to hold them both, but Cooper ambled up onto the limb across from her.

"Whatcha doing up here?"

"Just thinking. You know it's my favorite spot on the property."

"I know. It's got the best view, for sure."

"Where's Mom?"

"Last I saw, she was watching YouTube videos about beekeeping, so I had to get out of there. She's obsessed," he said, laughing.

"Yes, she is. I think she's excited to make something with Grandma's name on it. Maybe it makes her feel closer to her?"

"You're very astute, Evie. I think you're right about that."

"You know my Dad is coming tomorrow?"

He nodded. "I heard. Are you excited?"

She shrugged her shoulders. "I want to be, but I also don't want to be disappointed."

Cooper eyed her carefully. "Are you nervous about seeing him again?"

"I think so. I just don't know why he's coming. I don't know what he wants from me. And I know it's going to upset Mom when he gets here."

"I know you must be really freaking out about this, but remember you're just a kid. None of this is your fault or your responsibility. The way your dad has acted isn't a reflection on you."

She shrugged her shoulders. "That's what Mom said but why would he leave me like that? I mean, if he really wanted me, wouldn't he have stayed in touch?"

"You know, adults are weird. We don't always make a whole lot of sense, especially us guys. We have a hard time showing our feelings, and sometimes we make mistakes."

"I guess so. I won't really know what to think until I see him. I have had all these dreams over the years about having a dad again."

"I bet. It's hard, I'm sure. But your mom loves you, your aunt Mia loves you. Everything will work out fine."

She smiled. "Thanks, Cooper. You're always so nice to me."

"Everybody should be nice to you. You deserve that. You're a good kid."

"Sometimes…"

"Let's not talk about it…" he said, laughing.

"You know, it's getting harder and harder to sit up here in this tree."

"Oh yeah? Why's that?"

"I think I've rubbed most of the bark off of this limb, and I'm starting to get splinters on my rear end."

Cooper let out a loud laugh that echoed off into the distance. "I bet that feels great."

"Yeah, it doesn't. But I love being up here. I don't know what to do."

"I suppose you could build a treehouse," he said, offhandedly.

"You really think so?"

"Well, I was sort of joking, but you could do something like that. Maybe not an enclosed treehouse because you're not eight years old…"

"But some kind of treehouse?"

"What about some kind of large deck area? You could come up here, lay down and read a book? Listen to music? Look at the clouds and dream about boys?"

Evie giggled. "What makes you think I dream about boys?"

"Because you're a living, breathing teenage girl?" he said, pointing at her.

"So maybe you'd help me build something?"

"Of course! As long as your mother is okay with it. I certainly don't want to be in the doghouse with her. She might send those bees after me."

"Cool. Thanks, Cooper. I can't wait!"

Cooper started scooting back toward the trunk of the tree so he could climb down. "I'll start drawing something up. Well, I better get back before your mother notices I'm missing."

"Thanks for the talk. It made me feel better."

He looked up at her and smiled. "I'm glad. See you tomorrow!"

As she watched him carefully make his way to the ground, Evie couldn't help but be thankful for the new people in her life. Her aunt Mia, Cooper and even Travis, although she didn't know him too well. Her friend Dustin at school. Some of her teachers that she actually liked. Her school bus driver who always pretended not to notice that she had an open container of Coca-Cola in her hand every morning.

She would've never imagined that Carter's Hollow could have felt like home, but now she couldn't imagine any other place would feel that way. And her biggest concern was that her father was coming to try to take her away from there. And on that point, she would fight.

CHAPTER 4

$\mathcal{M}$ ia sat out on the back deck, her cardigan sweater pulled tight around her. Even though they were heading into spring soon, it was still pretty cold outside, especially up in the mountains.

It was her favorite time of day, the sun starting to disappear behind the mountains beyond, leaving in its wake wisps of orange and pink across the sky. Ever since she was a little kid, she had adored watching the sunsets in the mountains. Each one was different, no matter how many times she saw it. It was like God created a brand new painting night after night, and it just never got old.

Since her lunch with Travis and Sam, she hadn't been able to think about anything else. Dinner had just been going through the motions, as she wondered where Travis was. He normally came over for dinner, but he had been so wrapped up in Sam's visit that she hadn't seen much of him lately.

As a grown adult woman, she tried her best not to allow petty jealousy to creep into her heart, but for some reason she just couldn't help it. All of those years apart from Travis had been painful, as much as she didn't want to admit it to herself at the time. The thought that this woman, who he was apparently going to New York City with, could come between them made her sick to her stomach.

But the last thing she was going to do was admit it out loud to Travis. No, she would keep those thoughts to herself. Nothing good could come from him knowing how weak-minded she was, being worried about someone that she had only just met. Aside from that, she didn't want him to think that she didn't trust him. She did. Or at least she thought she did.

"Hey, sis," Kate said, as she walked out onto the deck, a large cup of coffee between her hands, warming them. "Do you want me to bring you a cup?"

"No thanks. I won't be out here much longer. Once that sun goes down, I get chilled to the bone." Mia pulled her cardigan even tighter, wishing she hadn't chosen the one that had the big holes, allowing more air to touch her petite body.

Kate sat down in the Adirondack chair next to her, took a long sip of her coffee and sighed. "It's a beautiful sunset tonight, isn't it?"

"It sure is."

They sat there silently for a few more moments

before Kate looked over at her sister. "Are you okay?"

"Yeah. Just a little melancholy tonight."

"Melancholy?"

"It was Momma's favorite word."

"I didn't know that. Interesting."

"She said it was a sad word but it had a beautiful poetic sound to it. She actually used it a lot."

"So she was often feeling melancholy?"

"I suppose I never thought about that, but I guess so. Probably missing our father."

"Where is Dad anyway?"

"I'm not sure. After dinner, I think he went upstairs. Maybe he decided to turn in early tonight," Mia said, leaning her head back against the chair and looking up at the sky. It wouldn't be long before it would be filled with stars, something she loved about living in the mountains. In the big city, all of the artificial lighting kept you from being able to see the beauty of the night sky, but up here she could see everything. When there weren't any clouds, it was like being out in the universe, floating around in the darkness.

"So, why are you feeling melancholy?" Kate asked, taking another sip of her coffee.

"Honestly, it's not worth talking about. It's silly, really."

"It's obviously bothering you. If you want to talk, you know I'm always here."

Mia nodded. "I know. And I appreciate it more than you realize. But, Momma always taught me that the more I focused on something, the more that I would attract it to myself. No sense in focusing on negative stuff."

Kate chuckled. "You're making her sound like some kind of New Age guru."

"She just said that I had to pay attention to my thoughts and my words because whatever I put out there would only swing around and come back to me."

"Wise woman."

"What about you? I heard that sigh when you came out here."

"Well, unlike you I'm willing to talk about all of the negative thoughts rolling around in my brain tonight. Brandon will be here tomorrow."

"Oh, I totally forgot about that. You must be a basket case."

Kate shrugged her shoulders. "Honestly, I don't know how to feel. I'm afraid he's going to step out of his car, and I'm just going to run across the driveway and kick him in the shin."

That made Mia laugh. "That sounds like a fantastic plan."

"I don't think it would endear me to my daughter, though. I think she's really excited about seeing her dad, although probably really anxious. We haven't talked about it much, but Cooper said he had a chat with her about it earlier today."

"Oh yeah? How do you feel about that?"

"She and Cooper have gotten really close over the last few months. I don't have any problem with her

him that couldn't help but think about Charlene and the wonderful love affair they'd had over the years. He missed her. It didn't make him feel guilty to think about her. After all, she was gone, and he had been married to Sylvia for years. But the love that he shared with Charlene was different. Timeless. Special. Something that was hard to duplicate. There would forever be a hole in his heart that no one could fill but her. It didn't mean he loved Sylvia any less. It just meant that their love was different.

He and Charlene had been soulmates, no doubt. Even as teenagers, he knew that she was "the one", but when their parents had intervened and separated them, he had felt adrift on an open sea for so long.

Then when they'd had the chance to reconnect, It was one of the most magical times of his life. And again, she was gone.

Now she was really gone. And even though he hadn't seen her in decades, there had been a grieving process after he found out. He supposed that some-where in the back recesses of his heart, he had expected they would one day be together again. But when cancer had taken her away, that option was gone.

So, sometimes he came to the B&B to see his daughters, of course. But other times he came because he was still missing Charlene deep down in his heart and just wanted to feel her presence. Her wisdom. Her love.

She had been the kind of person that never judged anyone and allowed everybody to be themselves. She was the least critical person he'd ever met in his life, including himself. She gave the best hugs, obviously made the best sweet tea and could win just about any argument.

She had a gentle way about her, a calming effect on his soul. He missed her in a way he hadn't expected after so many years, and there was nothing to do about it. No way to scratch that itch. So he sat there, staring out over the water, wondering what Charlene would be saying to him right now.

This secret he was keeping, what would she tell him to do? What would she want him to do?

"I didn't know you were out here. Want me to leave you alone?" Kate asked from the other end of the dock.

He smiled. "Of course not. Come join me."

She pulled the other chair over close to him and sat down, pulling a blanket around her shoulders that she had brought from the living room. The nights were getting colder and Jack could feel it in his bones.

"What are you doing out here so late?" she asked.

He picked up his insulated thermos full of coffee, took a sip and cleared his throat. "I don't know. I just like coming out here and listening to the silence. It's never as quiet in the world as it is up in the mountains late at night beside the lake."

"Yes, it's a great place to get away and think for a while."

"I can go inside if you need some time?"

She shook her head. "No. I would prefer your company to just sitting out here alone. "

"You seem a little melancholy tonight. Is something wrong?"

Kate looked at him for a long moment. "Melancholy?"

Jack laughed. "Sorry. Old habits. Your momma used to say that all the time."

"Yeah, Mia told me that. I've heard that word more today than I have in years."

"She was something else, that lady. I have to admit that sometimes I come here to the B&B because I get to feel her spirit around me. Of course, I'd never say that to Sylvia. She might take some offense, but I miss your momma."

Kate reached over and squeezed his knee. "From everything I understand, you two had the love of a lifetime."

"Yeah, for two people who never really got to be together very long, those old feelings will always be there. She was just one of a kind."

"That's what I've heard. I wish I had gotten to meet her. But, I know what you mean about this place allowing you to feel her spirit. Even though I didn't know her, I can somehow feel her here."

Jack nodded. "Trust me, she's here in that house but she's also here in these mountains and these trees. She's everywhere because her personality and ability to love people was so big that you can't contain her."

Kate smiled. "You should write poetry or something."

Jack shook his head and laughed. "Oh, I don't think so. Anyway, back to what I was asking. You seem a little sad tonight. How can I help?"

"Nobody can really help. I'm sure Mia told you that Evie's father is coming here in just a few hours. I should be asleep right now."

"Oh, is that tomorrow? I had totally forgotten. I'm not having a good feeling about this guy."

"Neither am I. I know him, and I know there's some ulterior motive to why he's coming here after all these years. He abandoned his daughter and now he suddenly wants to be back in her life? I don't buy it."

"I don't think anybody buys it, sweetie. We will all be watching him like a hawk, trust me. But, I think you're doing the right thing letting her have this time with him. I hope he doesn't break her heart."

Kate looked at him, her jaw tight. "If he breaks her heart, I'm going to break something of his. Possibly his face, but I'm open to suggestions."

Jack chuckled. "Do you feel that spunky spirit in you? That comes from your momma. She could smile so sweet, but she could turn around and cut you with a knife if you messed with anybody she loved. I like seeing those glimpses of her in you girls."

"So why are you out here so late at night? And don't tell me it's just because it's relaxing or you like the peace. It seems like something's going on since you got here. Let me help you."

Jack ruffled the hair on the top of her head like she was eight years old. "Darlin', I'm the dad. We don't tell our problems to our kids. Besides, it's nothing. No big deal. Just old man stuff."

He stood up and stretched his arms high over his head. He was beyond tired and knew he needed some sleep, especially if he was going to have to deal with possibly killing his daughter's ex-husband tomorrow.

"I think you're lying…" she said in a high-pitched sing-songy voice.

He leaned down and kissed the top of her head. "Good night, Katie girl. See you in the morning. I'll be sure to have my handgun on my side in case we need it when he gets here."

He walked off the dock and could hear Kate laughing off in the distance. It was only half a joke. If that guy messed with her or his granddaughter, he couldn't be sure of what he would do.

MIA WOKE up earlier than expected, feeling a sense of dread for her sister. She knew that Kate was very nervous about Brandon's arrival, and he would be there within the next hour.

Of course, she had also been kept up all night by her own crazy thoughts and worries about Travis. He had texted her late at night, told her he loved her and asked about her day. Everything seemed normal on his end, but she was also well aware that he would be leaving tomorrow to go to New York City with Sam.

She didn't know why this was bothering her so much. Cheating wasn't something she thought Travis would ever do, so that wasn't it. She supposed it was just a feeling of inferiority when she looked at Sam. How could Travis not find her attractive? How could Travis want to be with Mia and not with somebody like that who was obviously smart and beautiful?

Maybe she had just been stuck in the mountains too long. Maybe she thought that she should've gotten out into the world and done something big with her life, but her momma would tell her that running the bed-and-breakfast was big. Making people feel at home when they were away from home was a form of therapy, and she was doing good things. Sometimes, she could hear her mother's voice in her head, and it often provided comfort and clarity.

"Good morning," Kate said as she quickly trotted down the stairs. She had a look on her face, one that Mia hadn't seen before. Nervousness? Stress? It seemed like those two put together times one hundred.

"Good morning. I made you some eggs and there's a fresh pot of coffee."

"Where are our guests this morning?"

"They actually came down and had an early

breakfast… or I might have told them breakfast was an hour earlier than it was supposed to be just so we could get some time alone."

Kate looked at her, a grateful expression on her face. "Thank you. I really wasn't up for entertaining this morning. I've got so much adrenaline running through my body that I'm afraid I'm just going to take flight at some point."

"Where is Evie?"

"She just got out of the shower. I think she wants to make herself look pretty since her dad hasn't seen her in years. I swear, I don't think he'd recognize her if she walked right in front of him on the street."

Mia could see the muscles twitching in Kate's jawline. "Try to relax. I know it's hard, but you don't want to make Evie feel uncomfortable, right?"

"I know. I'm trying. I didn't sleep a wink last night. Spent a lot of time talking to Dad down by the dock."

"Dad was down there? Last night?"

"Yes, I found it a little odd too. I know he's keeping something from us. Maybe we should give Sylvia a call?"

"Let's not do that just yet. After all, if he wants us to know something, he'll tell us."

"You're right, as usual. Besides, I don't need to add any more stress to my life. Maybe he and Sylvia are having marriage problems, and I sure don't wanna get in the middle of that."

"Here, eat your eggs, drink your coffee and take some deep breaths."

Kate walked over to the table and sat down as Mia slid her food across. "Thanks for taking care of me. I was planning to just come down and get a yogurt because I don't think I have it in me to prepare a meal right now."

"That's what sisters are for," Mia said, smiling. "Besides, we all have your back. I know I've said it a thousand times, but we aren't going to let anything happen to Evie. She's just getting on her feet, and this guy is not going to mess that up, even if he is her father."

A few moments later, there was a knock at the front door. Kate froze in her seat, her eyes wide. "He's not supposed to be here for an hour."

Mia turned and looked out the front window. "Relax. It's just Travis. I don't know what he's doing here."

She walked out the front door and shut it behind her to give Kate some peace and quiet before everything began in an hour.

"Travis, I didn't expect to see you this morning. I thought you were taking some pictures over by the waterfall?"

"Yeah, there's been a change in plans," he said, leaning in to give her a quick peck on the lips. "I'm leaving town today instead of tomorrow."

"What? But I thought we were going to have dinner tonight before you left?"

"That was the plan, but Sam got called back for a meeting, and she thinks it would be great for me to be there. I'm actually going to meet with the president of the publishing company, and she's rarely in the office so this is a good opportunity for me to make some connections."

Mia couldn't help but feel sick to her stomach. "Oh. Well, I guess that's a good thing for you then."

"Are you okay with this?" he asked, looking at her carefully.

"Of course. I want what you want," she said, sounding like she was reading from a script. Surely he wasn't buying this, only it appeared that he was.

"You're so amazing, Mia. I really appreciate your support in this. I'm a little bit nervous."

In that moment, she realized how silly she was being. She hadn't even given any thought to how Travis might be feeling as he was about to embark on something so huge. Instead of feeling proud or excited for him, she had been stuck in her own mind, worrying about petty things that weren't even real. She felt terrible, but at least she could salvage the situation without him knowing just how immature she was being.

"I'm so proud of you. And I'm here for you one-hundred percent. I can't wait to see you when you get back, and I know you will make a great impression on the president of the company." She leaned in and pulled him into a tight hug, pressing her cheek to his chest. Mia drank in the smell of his cologne, hoping it would hold her over until he got back.

"It won't be long. And I promise when I get home, we will go out to a nice dinner and I'll tell you everything."

She pulled back and looked up at him. "I'm going to hold you to that. I've missed you lately."

"I've missed you too. I know this came out of the blue, and I promised not to leave again…"

"You're not leaving. You're going on a short trip. We will be back together again very soon."

"And please tell Kate that I hope everything goes well when her ex-husband gets here. I wish I could be here for back-up, but let her know I'm here in spirit."

Mia nodded. "Don't worry, she's got plenty of people to stand in the gap for her today."

"Oh, I know," he said, laughing. "That guy is not going to get by you, Cooper and your dad. I kind of feel sorry for him."

Mia squinted her eyes. "Don't feel sorry for him."

"I'm going to miss you. I'll call you tonight as soon as I get to my hotel. "

"I can't wait to hear from you," she said, holding his hands and smiling up at him.

"I love you, Mia." He leaned down and pressed his lips to hers for a long moment before turning and walking down the stairs.

"I love you too!" she called to him as she waved. He climbed into his truck and drove up the driveway and out of sight.

CHAPTER 5

Kate stood in the kitchen, nervously wiping down the counter as she waited for the inevitable knock at the door. Evie was sitting on the sofa, pretending to look at her phone, but Kate knew she was anxiously awaiting the arrival of her father. She and Evie hadn't really talked a lot about it in recent days because she didn't really want to pry or say something she shouldn't. She wasn't sure if her daughter was excited, anxious or scared. Maybe she should have asked more questions or shown more of an interest, but she figured that her daughter would come to her if she wanted to talk about it.

Mia was still upstairs getting ready for the day, but probably also licking her wounds with the fact that Travis had left a day early. She knew her sister was worried about losing Travis again, but she just didn't have the mental strength to talk to her either. Right now, everything was focused on making sure that her ex-husband didn't break her daughter's heart all over again.

"Hey. He's not here yet?" Cooper said as he slipped in through the back door. He was talking quietly, obviously not wanting to upset Evie. She now had her headphones in, probably blasting music to distract herself. The level of tension in the air was thick, like a smoky, hazy fog.

"No, not yet. But I expect him any minute. I'm sure he flew in this morning and is probably getting a rental car."

"And how are you?" Cooper asked, as he slid his hands around her waist. She put her hands on his chest and looked up into his genuine eyes. Kate was so thankful to have a different kind of man in her life now, someone strong and stable who would be there for her and her daughter no matter what. She had watched Cooper working to sketch out the perfect treehouse platform for Evie the day before, and it'd made her heart melt. She wasn't his daughter, but he always treated her like she was an important part of his life anyway.

"Nervous. Anxious. Slightly homicidal?"

Cooper laughed. "Maybe I should watch you more than I'm going to watch him."

"Maybe so. I'm just trying really hard not to say or do anything that will upset my child. Her emotional and mental well-being is far more important than me getting to say some things to Brandon that I really want to say."

"You're a great mom, Kate. I know you'll do the

right thing, and we will work together to protect her."

As if on cue, she heard a car door shut outside. Evie looked at her, her eyes wide. "Is that him?" She had no idea how she even heard the sound with her headphones in her ears.

Kate walked across the room and looked out the front window, peeking between the wooden plantation shutters. "It looks like it's him."

Evie stood up and pressed her hands down the front of her black skirt. She had worn one of the only skirts she owned, a pair of black flats and a red blouse that Kate had bought her for a wedding they went to a year ago.

"How do I look?" Evie asked, a slight smile on her face.

Kate walked over to her and ran her fingers down the side of Evie's hair. "You look beautiful, as you always do. And your father's not going to care how you look. He wants to see you because you're you."

"Thanks, Mom."

A moment later, there was a knock at the door. Kate stepped back a few feet, Cooper's hand on her lower back. "This is your moment, honey. Go ahead and answer it."

Evie sucked in a deep breath and then blew it out before walking to the front door. When she opened it, a flood of memories hit Kate like a ton of bricks. She hadn't seen Brandon in years, even getting rid of their wedding photos so she didn't have to look at him. She thought she'd never have to see him again since he had basically abandoned their daughter. Never did she assume he would be walking her down the aisle at her wedding or sitting in the waiting room one day when she was having their first grandchild, but here he was. Standing at her front door. In that moment, she was thankful she didn't know where Mia kept the shotgun.

"Evie?"

"Hey, Dad." The conversation was awkward. Stilted. A little bit canned. It made Kate feel uncomfortable for her daughter, but she wasn't going to say anything.

"You look so grown up," he said. Kate wanted to yell out, *"I guess so because you haven't seen her in years!"* but she refrained.

"It's been a long time. Do you want to come in?"

Brandon nodded, obviously nervous. He looked quite different than the last time she'd seen him. He was thinner, not quite as tan as he normally was. His formerly thick, dark hair had thinned out quite a bit over the years. He was wearing a pair of jeans and a simple polo shirt, his normal attire. Brandon had never been one to get into fashion, and he seemed to be stuck in the same time warp from the last time she'd seen him.

"Hi, Kate. It's good to see you. You look well," he said, still sounding extremely awkward. She just stared at him, no words coming out of her mouth. She didn't respond, welcome him to her home or say anything. She felt frozen.

"Hey. I'm Cooper." She was thankful to have a boyfriend who stepped up in that moment, obviously realizing she was stunned like a deer in the headlights.

"Nice to meet you." Brandon stood there for a moment longer than necessary looking at Kate, probably wondering if she'd gone mute or something.

"Come sit down, Dad. I want to hear how you've been."

Brandon walked over and sat down next to Evie on the sofa, about three feet of space between them. Kate could tell that her daughter was still very hesitant, as she should've been. No girl should ever have to feel like her father was a stranger, like she needed to sit down in her living room to catch up with him after years of time apart.

"I just can't believe how grown up you look," he said.

"Well, it has been a lot of years. You look a little different too."

Kate felt an overwhelming sense of sadness as she listened to their conversation. They had been so close when Evie was a little girl. Kate couldn't deny that they'd had a tight relationship, a typical father daughter bond. That's why she had been so shell-shocked when Brandon had decided to cut her out of his life for reasons she would never understand.

And then he had married Kara and runoff to Mexico, having a new family of his own. How did a parent do that? How did he just cast Evie aside like she didn't matter? How could he sleep at night knowing he had a daughter out there somewhere who didn't know what she had done wrong to deserve losing her father?

Not wanting to interfere in her daughter's reconnection with her father, Kate quietly walked back into the kitchen, Cooper following behind her. They walked out onto the back deck, shutting the door as softly as possible.

"You okay?" Cooper asked.

"No. I feel worse than I thought I would. I don't even know why I couldn't say any words. It just seemed like none of the words I had on the tip of my tongue were appropriate for the moment."

"It's going to be alright. Your daughter is smart, and she will know how to handle her father. You've already raised her to be a strong young lady."

Kate slid her arms around his waist and pressed her cheek to his chest, sinking into him. Right now, she just needed somebody to be her rock.

"I hope you're right. I feel like I'm just serving her up on a silver platter so that he can hurt her all over again."

"You know, maybe he really does want to reconnect with her. Maybe he'll surprise you."

Kate looked up at him and chuckled. "I know you're trying to see the positive in this, but you don't know Brandon. There's something else going on here, and I intend to find out what it is."

MIA WALKED up the stairs with Brandon following behind, holding a suitcase in his hand. She couldn't believe the man was staying at their B&B. She feared that Kate might get up in the middle of the night and "accidentally" smother him while he slept.

"Wow, these stairs are pretty steep," he said. For somebody at such a young age, only in his early forties, he sure was out of breath. It wasn't like he was overweight or anything, so Mia couldn't quite figure it out. Maybe he just didn't get much exercise in Mexico.

"Yeah? Well none of us have any problems with them." She sort of wanted to turn around and push him down the stairs on behalf of her sister and niece. But she thought better of it, not wanting to spend the rest of her life in jail. After all, that would mean Travis may ride off into the sunset with Sam.

"I see," Brandon said, his voice monotone.

"You'll be in room four. It overlooks the lake, in case you want to jump out of the window at some point." She flipped on the light, stepped back and crossed her arms, leaning against the door frame.

Brandon walked past her and put his suitcase on the bed before turning around. "Do you have some sort of a problem with me?"

Mia's mouth dropped open. "How long do you have?"

"Look, we've never met. You don't know the first thing about me, and it's not very welcoming the way that you're acting."

"I am Kate's sister."

"Oh. I see. Yes, Evie told me that Kate found her sister on some Internet site. Who knew that her mother got around like that?"

It took every ounce of restraint that Mia had not to lunge forward and strangle him with her tiny little hands. "You really need to think about your words," she warned. "Around here, we don't take too kindly to people talking about our mothers, and I'm a very straight shot."

"Are you threatening to shoot me?" he asked, incredulously.

Mia walked forward, looked up at him and pointed her finger. "Listen up, buddy. That's my sister and my niece down there. And you're in my mother's house. You will either be respectful, or I will call the local sheriff and have you carted out of here so fast it'll make your head spin."

Brandon held up his hands. "Calm down, lady. I'm just here to see my daughter. I don't need any drama from you or your sister."

She felt like her face was going to explode. A flush feeling rushed through her body, and she felt like she would be able to easily lift a car off of someone right now.

"I don't know what my sister ever saw in you."

"Well, I don't know what I ever saw in her either, so that makes two of us."

"Dinner is at seven." She turned to start walking toward the door.

"What about lunch?"

"You're on your own," she said before slamming the door.

She turned to walk down the hallway but then heard Evie. She was poking her head out of her bedroom door.

"So you met my dad?" she asked, softly.

Mia cleared her throat and tried really hard not to look like an angry wolverine. "I did. I just got him settled in his room."

Evie walked out of her room and toward her aunt. "What did you think about him?"

"Honey, it doesn't matter what I think. He's your dad, and I hope that you get what you need out of this time together."

Evie eyed her carefully, like she wanted to say something else, but she didn't. She probably didn't want to hear the real, honest answer that Mia was going to give her.

"I hope Mom is okay. She didn't even greet him when he came in."

Mia rubbed Evie's arm. "This is hard, but she'll be okay. All she wants is for you to have a good experience with this. Just focus on that. Get the answers you need and build the relationship you want. We are all supporting you."

Evie smiled. "Thanks, Aunt Mia."

As Mia turned and walked down the stairs, she wondered just how much trouble she might get in if she disconnected the brakes on Brandon's rental car.

~

"So, you like living here?" Brandon asked as he and Evie walked down the long driveway. She had invited him to come with her to check the mail, even though she could've just as easily taken the golf cart.

"I love it, actually."

He looked around, like he was taking it all in. "I never pictured you or your mother living in a place like this."

She looked at him. "A place like this?"

"Well, I mean, it's pretty remote and not near any cities or big shopping areas."

"I don't really like to shop," she said, pointing out yet another thing her own father should know about her.

"Oh. I didn't realize that."

She wanted to lash out and say why he didn't know it, but she held her tongue. "I prefer hiking and climbing trees around here."

Brandon chuckled. "I don't know many teenage girls who like that kind of stuff."

"Well, maybe I'm not like other teenage girls. In fact, that's my favorite tree right there." She pointed across the driveway at the large tree.

"Oh, is it now?" he said, out of breath from the walk. Evie found it odd that he seemed so winded, but maybe he just wasn't used to such a long walk in the cold weather. After all, Mexico wasn't exactly a chilly place to live.

Evie walked toward the tree and noticed Cooper was sitting up there. "Oh, hey, Cooper! I didn't see you up there. I was just showing Dad my favorite tree."

Cooper waved and then slowly climbed down, jumping the last six feet or so. "Hey. I was just sketching some things out."

"You're sketching in a tree? Don't you have a job or something?" Brandon asked, condescension dripping in his voice.

Cooper straightened, and Evie was afraid he might just sock her father right in the nose, and she couldn't blame him. He was acting like a jerk.

"Dad! You're being rude."

"It's okay, Evie. He's new around here and doesn't understand how we act."

"How you act?"

Cooper smiled slightly. "How we have good southern manners. How we sometimes think things but don't say them. Anyway, for your information, I do have a job. Actually, I have a business. I'm a contractor. And your daughter loves this tree, so I'm building her a treehouse."

"A treehouse? Evie, aren't you a little old for that?"

She sighed. This wasn't going well. "It's more of a platform. And it makes me happy, so Cooper offered."

"Well, I guess whatever floats your boat…" he said, turning back toward the house.

Evie smiled at Cooper. "Sorry about that."

"It's okay. You better catch up with him. I'll show you my sketch later."

She waved as she trotted off to catch up with Brandon.

"You know, Evie, a girl your age should have tons of friends and be going to parties, not climbing up in trees and sitting alone. Doesn't your mom encourage you to be social?"

"I am social. I have friends at school. But, life is different around here. Slower."

"And boring?"

She stopped in her tracks and put her hands on her hips. "Why did you even come here?"

"Excuse me?"

"Why are you here, Dad? After all these years, you show up without any explanation of what you want. And you keep making smart comments about my new life. I'll have you know I love it here! I love the mountains and the lake and the rivers. I love my new aunt and my grandfather and Cooper."

"Cooper isn't your father," he said under his breath.

"And you haven't been my father in years!"

"Evie…" he said, holding up his hand.

"No! You need to listen to me, for once. You left me behind, Dad. Left me without even caring that I would be hurt. Started a new family. Forgot I even existed."

"I never forgot you."

"Well, I must have missed all of those phone calls and texts you sent. Or the cards. Or maybe I wasn't home when you visited?"

Brandon stepped forward and put his hands on

her upper arms, the first fatherly thing he'd done since he had gotten there.

"I'm sorry. You're right. I haven't been there, and I have no right to judge your life now. I don't even know that Cooper guy, so I shouldn't have been so rude to him. "

"Thank you," she said.

"Look, I want this to work. I want us to rebuild our relationship. Don't you remember how much fun we had when you were a little girl? When we used to go fishing at the shore? When we would play frisbee at the park?"

Evie struggled not to allow her eyes to fill with tears. She was tough, like her mother, and she didn't like for people to see her sweat. "I remember. And I wish it could be that way again."

"It can. That's why I'm here. I want to reconnect with you. I hope you'll give me that chance."

She stepped back and crossed her arms. "Fine, but you have to stop being so critical. I love this place. It's my home, and I hope to stay around here forever. I feel like I finally found where I'm supposed to be."

"I'm glad. All I want is for you to be happy."

She paused for a moment. "How would you like to go fishing before dinner?"

"I'd love that."

As they turned and walked back toward the house, Evie wondered whether they would really be able to mend their relationship. She wasn't sure, but she hoped so. As much as she was angry at her father, she loved him. She wanted their old relationship again.

~

"I'm so glad you got here safely" Sam said as Travis opened his hotel room door.

"What are you doing here? I thought we weren't meeting until tomorrow morning?"

"Well, I thought you might be hungry for dinner so I brought…" She held up a bag full of Chinese food containers. "I remember how much you loved the Mongolian beef at Golden Dragon. So I grabbed some and extra eggrolls and headed over here. I hope you don't mind?"

He actually did mind. He had just gotten to the hotel from the airport a half hour before, and he was tired and ready for a shower and a nice soft bed. Plus, he really wanted to call Mia and hear her voice. But, he didn't want to offend Sam and possibly ruin his chances with this new opportunity.

"Sure. Come on in. I'm famished."

Sam smiled broadly and walked past him into the hotel room. She set everything down on the round wooden table by the sliding glass doors that led to the terrace overlooking the city. If there was one thing he would give her, it was that she had wonderful taste in hotels. He didn't know how much this place was costing per night, but the publishing company was paying for it.

"How many eggrolls do you want?" she asked as she started pulling everything out of the bags.

"I'll start with one and see how it goes," he said, laughing.

For the next hour, they ate and talked and laughed about old times. He and Sam had worked together quite a bit over the years on all kinds of projects.

"Do you remember that sketchy fried chicken place? The one where we had to take the pictures and found a feather still sticking out of one of the pieces?" Sam asked.

"I'm glad we're finished eating. If you had brought that up while I was eating that sesame chicken, I might have thrown up," Travis said, wiping his mouth.

"Man, we had some fun times back then. Even though we made next to no money, I kind of miss it sometimes."

"Yeah, well I don't. Taking pictures of hamburgers and french fries wasn't exactly what I had planned for my future."

She smiled. "What do you have planned for your future, Travis? Because I can't help but notice that it seems like you're regressing."

He looked at her, his eyebrows furrowed together. "What do you mean?"

"Well, no offense, but that little town you're living in isn't exactly a great place to build a fabulous career. You need to come back to the city for that."

"No thanks. I don't ever want to move away from Carter's Hollow again."

She shook her head. "Travis, you're one of the most talented photographers I know. But, if you're living so far away from all of the opportunities, I fear that you won't ever be able to live out your dreams."

"Doing the photos for this book is all I'm interested in right now. I love my home, and I love Mia. I promised her I'd never leave again."

She smiled. "Is that what this is all about? A promise to Mia?"

"Somewhat."

"Let me ask you a question. If Mia agreed to move to New York City with you, or even to Atlanta, would you go?"

He stood up and picked up the paper bag full of empty Chinese food boxes. He crushed it and walked across the room, stuffing it into the trashcan.

"It doesn't really matter because it's never going to happen. She has a life there, and we were apart for too many years for me to ever consider leaving again."

"Well, if there's one thing I've learned is that you should never say never."

Travis laughed and shook his head. "Maybe you should be in sales, Sam. You'd probably be very good at it."

"That's not the first time I've heard that." As she stood up with her soda in her hand, she tripped over the leg of the table, knocking it onto the wooden surface. The splash ricocheted and hit Travis all over his T-shirt.

"Oh my gosh! I'm so sorry!"

"No problem. I was about to change clothes anyway. This is a little bit sticky, so let me go take a quick shower and change clothes."

"Okay, I'll wait here."

CHAPTER 6

Mia definitely wasn't looking forward
to this very awkward dinner. She
expected that Kate might lunge across the table at
Brandon at some point, and they may have to call
the sheriff out to calm down the commotion.

As she stirred the mashed potatoes, she thought
about how hard this must be on her sister. This man
who had abandoned her child all those years ago
would now be sitting across the table, and there was
little she could do. If Kate didn't keep her composure, she risked losing her relationship with her
daughter. Thankfully, their only guests had left that
morning and the new ones wouldn't arrive for a few
more days.

Even though she knew she should only be
thinking about her sister's situation, she found her
mind wandering. Had Travis made it safely to New
York City? She hadn't heard from him yet, and it was

a little concerning since he should've landed at least two hours ago.

She tried not to think about it as she scooped the mashed potatoes into the bowl. Everybody would be coming down soon, and the yeast rolls weren't quite ready yet.

Unable to stop herself from worrying, she decided to go ahead and give Travis a call. "Do you mind finishing this up? I just want to make a quick phone call."

Kate, who seemed lost in her own thoughts, nodded. "Sure. And I'll check the rolls in a minute."

Mia pulled her phone out of her apron pocket and stepped out onto the back deck to get some privacy. She dialed Travis's number and waited for him to answer. Normally, he was pretty good about answering on the first ring, especially when he saw it was her. But this time, it had already rang three times before it was answered.

"Hello?" Mia froze. Was that Sam's voice? Why was she answering Travis's phone? Had he been hurt?

"Sam?"

"Oh, hi, Mia."

"Is Travis okay?"

"Of course. Why do you ask?"

"Well, I know he landed a couple of hours ago. I expected to hear from him…"

"Oh. Sorry. That's my fault."

"Your fault?"

"I showed up at his hotel room with a bag full of

Chinese food," she said with a chuckle. "He never could say no to the eggrolls at Golden Dragon."

Mia's stomach churned. This felt way too familiar. Way too intimate. "Oh. Well, he does love his Chinese food. Listen, is he around so I can chat with him for a moment?"

There was a long pause before Sam spoke. "Actually... He's taking a shower."

"He's taking a shower? While you're there?"

She giggled. "I spilled a bit of my drink on his shirt."

Mia felt her pulse rate skyrocketing. What was going on in that hotel room so many miles away? "Can you ask him to give me a call?"

"Of course!" Sam's level of enthusiasm was a little too much for Mia right now.

"Thanks."

As she ended the call, she felt like she wanted to throw up. Why was this bothering her so badly? Was she overreacting or was it really strange that her boyfriend had another woman in his hotel room, and he was taking a shower?

She tried to gather her composure before walking back into the kitchen. Kate was going to need her help at dinner, and she had to get focused.

KATE HAD NEVER FELT such an internal struggle in her entire life. There she sat, at the other end of the table from the person she disliked most in the world.

Every so often, he would make eye contact with her and then quickly look away, probably worried that she might just jump straight over the table and smother him in a bowl of mashed potatoes.

"So, how was the fishing today?" Jack asked, only looking at Evie and completely ignoring Brandon.

"Pretty good. I caught a couple of bass and threw them back, of course."

"Good girl. One day we'll have a fish fry out there."

Evie smiled. "Dad also caught a fish. It wasn't quite as big as mine, but pretty good," she said as she looked over at Brandon.

"You just need better bait," he said before taking a bite of his roll.

"Better bait? I'll have you know that cut up hotdogs is one of the best bait you can use," Jack said, glaring at Brandon.

"That must be a southern thing because we don't use cut up hotdogs as our bait up north. It was kind of weird."

"Let me tell you something..." Jack said, rising up out of his chair a little.

"Why don't we change the subject?" Mia said loudly. Jack eased back down into his seat.

"Sorry. I didn't realize discussing bait would be so controversial," Brandon said, laughing under his breath.

"So, Dad, I understand I have a brother and sister?" Evie suddenly interjected.

Brandon looked a little surprised that she had

brought it up at a table full of people that included her mother, grandfather and aunt. Of course, Cooper was also there, sitting silently and trying to stay out of the crossfire.

"You're right. You have a little sister named Abigail, and she's seven. And you have a little brother named Elijah and he's nine."

"Do they know about me?"

"Of course. I've shown them pictures. They'd like to meet you one day. Kara just wants to wait until they're a little older."

The whole thing feels so very awkward to Kate. Why did her daughter have to ask about her siblings? Why didn't she already know them? And why couldn't they know her now?

"Why can't they meet me now?"

Brandon cleared his throat, obviously uncom-fortable. He reached over and touched her hand. "Kara just thinks they're a little too young to know the situation."

"What situation?" Evie pressed.

"That your father had a wife before Kara. And that he left his kid behind," Kate blurted out. Evie glared at her. "Sorry," Kate mouthed.

"So, what are you doing for a living, Brandon?" Jack asked, his voice monotone.

Brandon looked down at his plate as if he was nervous. Kate figured he was still in the same line of work, doing electrical projects for large office build-ings. He'd learned the business from his father many years ago.

"Actually, I'm not working right now. Taking some time off to reassess."

Kate wasn't buying it. Something else was going on. Maybe he and his wife had separated or divorced? Maybe his other kids didn't have anything to do with him, so he was coming for the one child that might still be interested.

"You're not working? I'm surprised. You made really good money doing all of the electrical work on those buildings." Even though he'd made great money over the years, he'd never sent any to his daughter. Kate could've gone after him for spousal support and certainly child support, but her pride had gotten in the way, and she'd never gone to court. Sometimes she wished that she did, if for no other reason than to punish him for walking out on his daughter.

"Yeah, I'm not sure I want to keep doing that. It's pretty physically taxing."

"You're still a young man. I worked until just a few years ago," Jack said in true macho man fashion.

"The food is really good. It's been a while since I had a home-cooked American meal," Brandon said, obviously changing the subject.

"Thanks," Kate said.

Brandon looked up at her, his head tilted to the side. "Don't tell me you cooked this? You never could figure your way around a kitchen."

"You know what, buddy?" Cooper started to say. Kate smiled and squeezed his hand.

"It's okay. Nothing he says affects me anymore."

79

"Mom has become a really great cook. She's even able to make some southern food."

"Sorry," he said, obviously not actually meaning it. "It's just amazing how some things change, I guess."

"Well, I guess they do when you let so many years pass and don't see the people that you supposedly love, like your daughter." Mia said before slapping her hand over her mouth to try to stop any further words from spitting out.

Brandon smiled, but not in a happy way. Kate could tell he was irritated, maybe embarrassed? He wiped his mouth and then put his napkin on the table before sliding his chair out and standing up.

"Look, I know there's only one person at this table who actually wants me here, and that's enough for me. I came to see my daughter, and nothing that any of you say is going to ruin that for me. If you'll excuse me, I'm going to go up to my room to make a phone call."

He turned and walked out of the room and up the stairs. As soon as he was out of earshot, Evie turned and glared, individually, at every person at the table.

"Why are y'all doing this? I thought everybody wanted me to make an effort with him? I can't do that if you run him off!"

"I'm so sorry for what I said. It just came out," Mia said, reaching over and rubbing Evie's shoulder.

"And Grandpa, why are you being so hard on him?"

"Listen, I don't expect you to understand, but I look at him and see the man who left my granddaughter behind. That's a very hard thing to forgive."

"But isn't it up to me whether I forgive him or not? You guys are making this impossible!" Evie said, pushing her chair out aggressively before walking out of the room. She went out the front door, slamming it behind her.

Kate started to stand up to follow her. "Why don't you give her some time?" Cooper said. Kate sat back down in her chair.

"She's right, you know? The whole purpose of this visit is to give her whatever she needs from her father. But I can't help it. When I look at him, I just feel this rage well up inside of me. It brings up so many memories of wrapping her in my arms and rocking her while she cried about her father. Or all of those daddy-daughter dances where she stayed home and saw her friends' pictures on social media. I don't think he fully understands what he's done to her."

"Well, maybe you should have a conversation with him?" Mia suggested.

Kate laughed. "Are you kidding me? I've had tons of conversations with him on the phone. I don't think he cares."

"Then why is he here?" Jack asked.

"I wish I knew. There's something else going on, but I don't know what it is."

"Maybe you should call his wife," Cooper said.

"Call his wife? Why on earth would I do that?"

"Because she knows the real reason he's here."

Kate picked up her plate and walked over to the trashcan, raking the rest of it into the can and then putting her plate in the sink. "I have never spoken to that woman, and I don't think I want to. Besides, the chances of her actually telling me the truth are slim to none."

"Do you think so? I mean, if they split up she will probably tell you everything you ever wanted to know," Mia said.

"But if they're still together, she will tell him I called and we will have a big blowup right here in front of our daughter."

"Yeah, that might be true."

"All I can do is try to keep my mouth shut, let this play out and hope that whatever he's here for won't end up hurting Evie. Because if he hurts her again, he's not going to walk out of here on two legs," Kate said before walking out the back door to get some fresh air.

COOPER WALKED OUTSIDE and down toward the dock. He knew he would probably find Evie there. It was one of her favorite places, aside from the tree that she liked to sit in. He could see her silhouette standing at the edge of the water, her hands in the pockets of her hoodie. It was still quite cold outside, and he was looking forward to spring.

"You know, when I was a kid, I almost drowned in this lake."

"Really?"

"Yeah. Me and my buddies packed into a canoe and the thing toppled over. I was about twelve years old, and I wasn't a great swimmer. Actually, I'm still not the best swimmer."

"That must've been really scary."

"It was terrifying. There was just this feeling of paddling and paddling and never making any headway. No matter what I did, I just couldn't seem to get my head above water. The only way I made it to shore was that my friend's dad jumped in and lifted me up."

"Why are you telling me this?" she asked, still staring straight ahead.

"Because the adults in your life are supposed to lift you up, and what we did back there at the dinner table certainly wasn't that. I just wanted to apologize for my part."

She looked at him and nodded. "Thanks."

Cooper walked over and pulled the two Adirondack chairs closer to the edge before taking a seat. Evie waited a few moments and then sat down as well.

"Do you want to talk about it?"

She blew out a breath. "You know, it's not like I don't know what my dad has done. I know better than anyone. I cried so many times missing him, wondering what I'd done wrong to deserve for my own father to leave me behind. But, I'm trying to give him a second chance. I don't know if he really deserves it, but I'd like to know that I tried."

"Understandable. I think that's a very mature way of looking at it."

"I thought my mother wanted me to do this. I thought she understood, and aunt Mia too. But everybody is just attacking him, and it's going to ruin any chance that I have of creating a new relationship with him."

"Everybody felt terrible when you left the table. We're all going to try harder, Evie."

"OK. I hope so. I'm mad at him. But I also love him."

"He's your father. It's totally normal that you love him, even though he hasn't always made the best decisions."

She looked over at Cooper and smiled. "You know, sometimes I wish that you had been my father."

For a moment, Cooper felt like he might actually start crying. No one had ever said anything so nice to him. "Really?"

"Yeah. We get along well, and you treat my mother great. But, he's still my dad. And I feel like I have to try."

Cooper leaned forward and held one of her hands. "I'm here no matter what. And you have your mother, your aunt and your grandfather. Plenty of people love you and support you, so you do what you think is right."

They sat there, holding hands, staring out over

the lake for a few moments. Cooper didn't have any children of his own, but he had started to think of Evie like a daughter. And there was a part of him that was struggling not to put his hands around Brandon's neck for the way he had treated her. But, for now, he would sit and support her like a good dad would.

~

MIA WASHED her face and slipped on her nightgown. Going to bed early felt like the right thing to do given how crazy dinner had been. Plus, she was trying not to think about the fact that Travis still hadn't called her and that Sam had answered his phone.

She picked up her phone for the hundredth time and looked at it, checking to see if Travis had sent her a text message. No such luck. Deciding that she needed to relax a bit, she leaned over and turned on the hot water in her large clawfoot tub. She was going to soak in a bubble bath, listen to her favorite playlist and forget this day ever happened.

Just as she turned on the water, the phone vibrated on the counter next to her. She quickly turned the water off when she saw Travis's name on the screen.

"Hello?" she said, trying not to sound too excited to hear from him.

"Hey, babe! Sorry I'm so late calling you. My

flight got in a little late, and then I had to eat dinner and get settled in. "

Funny that he hadn't mentioned Sam. Mia wondered if Sam had even told him that she called. And it seemed very unlike him that he would just ignore her call and wait for another two hours to call her back.

"I'm glad to hear from you. I was getting a little worried."

"I'm sorry. The flight was a little bumpy, and it took me forever to find my luggage. But, I wanted to call and tell you how much I miss you already."

That made her feel better. Maybe he was telling the truth. Maybe eating dinner with Sam just wasn't that big of an event for him, so he hadn't mentioned it.

"I miss you too. Dinner was crazy tonight."

"Oh yeah? I bet. How is Kate handling everything?"

"Not great. None of us are. We sort of ganged up on Brandon over mashed potatoes."

Travis chuckled. "Well, he deserves it."

"Yes, he does. But we have to try to make it nice for Evie. It caused her a lot of stress, and she walked out on dinner."

"Oh no. I'm sorry to hear that. I just can't imagine abandoning my kid like he did."

Mia walked over and dipped her finger in the little bit of water that had accumulated in the tub. It was starting to get room temperature, and she was still looking forward to that hot bath.

SWEET TEA & HONEY BEES

"I don't understand it either. And then there's my dad. He's acting really strangely."

"You still haven't figured out why he's there?"

"No. He claims he's just here because he wants to see his daughters, but I have a feeling something else is going on. We thought about calling Sylvia, but we figured it's best to just let him tell us in his own time."

"Do you think they're having marriage trouble?"

" I don't know. I hope not. We love Sylvia."

"Well, I love *you*. And I can't wait to talk to you tomorrow after my meeting."

"Same here. I can't wait until you get home and we have some time together. It seems like ages since we've been able to just hang out."

"I know. But everything will be great soon. I just know it."

She smiled, the mere sound of his voice filling her heart. "You're going to do great. I hope everything goes well!"

"Thanks, honey. Listen, I'm exhausted. I'll give you a call tomorrow after my meeting, okay?"

"Okay. Good night."

"Good night."

As Mia ended the call and put her phone on the counter again, she still had to wonder why he never mentioned his dinner with Sam. She trusted Travis with all of her heart, but there was just something about that woman that left her feeling uneasy. Travis was so naïve, so trusting. What if this woman had other ideas about their relationship?

RACHEL HANNA

Trying to wipe the idea from her mind, she turned the water back on, poured in some liquid bubble bath and turned up her playlist. For tonight, she just needed to relax. She could deal with all of her worries again tomorrow.

CHAPTER 7

*K*ate stood on the front porch, eagerly awaiting the arrival of the truck. She never thought that getting boxes of bees would be so exciting to her, but there she was. She wasn't as excited about interacting with bees all the time, but she was thrilled to have another possible business to go with the B&B. She couldn't wait to release her first bottles of Sweet Charlene's Honey.

"Darrell said he would be here in just a few minutes," Jack said as he came out of the house. Darrell was one of Jack's oldest friends, and he just happened to be a very experienced beekeeper in the area.

"I'm so excited that we ended up ordering from him. I talked to him on the phone, and he seems like a really nice guy."

"Oh, he's a great guy. Eccentric, but very nice."

"Eccentric?"

"Well, let's just say Darrell is a bit of a hoarder.

He likes to collect things, and bees are one of those things. He also collects taxidermy and… get this… teapots."

"Teapots?" Kate said, laughing.

"Darrell's mother owned an antique store for fifty years. They used to go junkin', as he called it, and he developed a love for all kinds of things. Then, he went to this one property where the guy was a beekeeper, and that became his newest obsession."

"He told me he sells bees and all kinds of accessories to people all over the country."

"Oh that's definitely true. "

As they continued talking, Kate saw a truck coming down the driveway that she didn't recognize. "Is that him?"

"Looks like it. He's been driving a beat up old red Chevy truck for as long as I've known him," he said, laughing.

They walked down the stairs and onto the driveway. Darrell, one of the shortest men Kate had ever seen, jumped down out of the truck and walked over to them. He was bald, a little chubby and had huge black rimmed glasses. Not at all what she was expecting.

"Well, as I live and breathe! How're you doin', Jack?" he said, shaking his hand.

"Oh, I suppose I'm doing pretty good. This is my daughter, Kate."

"Nice to meet you, Kate. I've got you the best bunch of bees I've had in a while!"

"How do you know they're the best bunch?" Kate asked, laughing.

"Well, I do believe they have the best sounding buzz."

He turned and walked toward the truck, and Kate gave her dad a look. She wasn't sure if Darrell was being serious or pulling her leg.

"Now, I've got you everything you need right here to set up a successful beekeeping business. This right here is your protective suit, and I've got these rubber boots and some gloves. Now these are your nucs."

"Nucs?"

"Nucleus colonies. They're all ready to go inside this box. Now we might need to split some colonies at some point, and then we'll put them into these larger frames."

Darrell kept holding up different things, and Kate was trying to keep up. Right now she wished that she had brought a notebook and a pen.

"Don't worry, Kate. Darrell knows exactly what he's doing. He'll get all of this set up and show you how to do everything."

"And I also live just a few miles down the road. I'm happy to come over any time you need help. And I expect to get that first jar of Sweet Charlene's Honey. I love a good peanut butter and honey sandwich."

Kate crinkled her nose, but went back to smiling before Darrell looked her way. "No problem. I will set aside that first jar especially for you."

Darrell turned back to the truck. "Now you're gonna need these food grade buckets. Here's your strainer, horse hair brushes, hive tool, smoker…" As he started listing everything off, Kate suddenly felt extremely overwhelmed. What in the world had she gotten herself into?

∽

TRAVIS SAT NERVOUSLY at the conference table. The meeting had been going well, but a couple of the managers had stepped out to confer privately about his contract to take the pictures for the book. He was left alone sitting at the table with Sam, eying the large bowl of chocolate candy directly within his sight.

"I think things are going really well," she said, trying to reassure him.

"You think so? Why did they have to go have a private conversation? Maybe they are having second thoughts about me."

She reached across the large table and patted his hand. "You're overthinking it. Trust me, they love you."

"Well, I'm glad you're so sure of that because I'm not. I'm not even sure what I'm doing here, Sam. I'm just an old country boy who belongs in the foothills of the Blue Ridge mountains. Being back in New York City has me feeling like a fish out of water."

She laughed. "Travis, you act like you've never

been here before! You worked right here in the city for almost a decade. What's gotten into you?"

"I don't know." He leaned back in the chair and looked up at the ceiling. "I guess when I got back home, I never really wanted to leave again. This place feels foreign, like I've never been here in my life."

She shook her head. "You're too big for that town. There are photographers all over the world who would kill for an opportunity like this. I don't know why you don't see your potential."

He chuckled. "You've always seen a lot more in me than I do myself. And I appreciate that, I really do. But just because I *can* do something doesn't mean I *should*."

"Are you telling me that you're having second thoughts about the book deal?" she whispered.

"No. Not about the book deal. But, I have a feeling that you might think that I'm going to come back to the city, and that's just not where my future is.

"As I've said before, never say never," she said, a sly grin on her face. Before Travis could respond, the managers came back into the room.

"Sorry to keep you waiting for so long,"

The two men, Peter and Elliot, sat back down. Travis had forgotten how stiff conference rooms felt. There was a beautiful view of the city; well, as beautiful as cities could be. He never understood when people said they were beautiful. Buildings and concrete and honking horns had never appealed to him like the beauty of nature. That, he understood.

"Travis, we want you to know that we are so impressed with your artistic talent. Rarely do we see photographers with your skill level. With that being said, we would like to go ahead and offer you the position to take pictures for this book." Elliott slid the contract across the table, along with a fancy black pen.

Sam smiled broadly. "Congratulations, Travis!"

"Thank you. Truly, I appreciate you allowing me to do this. The Blue Ridge Mountains are my home, and being able to showcase them to the world in this book will be amazing." He looked down and quickly signed the contract since he'd reviewed it earlier in their meeting.

"We'd like you to get started as soon as possible. My assistant, Gabby, will get in touch with you by email over the next week or so to start coordinating the shots and schedule."

"That sounds amazing. Thank you, again," Travis said, standing up and shaking both of their hands.

A few moments later, he and Sam were back out on the busy sidewalk, surrounded by skyscrapers. He couldn't believe that his name was going to be on a book!

"Are you just stunned?" Sam asked, a big smile on her face.

"Stunned doesn't begin to cover it. I mean, I knew they wanted to talk to me about it but I wasn't really sure if I would get it. Thank you again for recommending me for this opportunity."

"I'm really happy for you, Travis. And, to celebrate I think we should go over to Le Maison bistro."

Travis's mouth dropped open. "Are you kidding me? That's one of the most expensive places in the city!"

"It's my treat as a congratulations! Do you remember when our boss came in from Los Angeles and took us there that one time? You had the filet mignon with the mushroom sauce on it?"

"I remember. And you had escargot which made me wanna throw up."

Sam laughed. "See? You do have some good memories of living in the city."

"I didn't say that I don't have good memories. I'm just saying I don't care to make any new ones here."

She smiled sadly and shook her head before raising her arm to flag a taxi. One stopped immediately in front of her which was no surprise because Sam was quite attractive. Any taxi driver was probably excited to have her in the backseat.

"Never say never," she repeated for the millionth time. "I have a little something I want to discuss with you at lunch." She climbed into the taxi, one of her long, bare legs still sticking out for a moment. The way she got into a vehicle was much like a supermodel getting into a limo. Although she was a beautiful woman, Travis had never had any interest. Mia had always been firmly implanted in his heart.

"You're not talking me into anything, Sam…" he

groaned as he joined her in the taxi and they took off into the crazy city traffic.

~

EVIE TOOK a long sip of her vanilla milkshake and swallowed it down. It was still pretty cold outside, but she could never resist a milkshake at the diner. "Does Mom know that you picked me up from school?"

"No. Was I supposed to tell her?" Brandon asked.

"She's going to wonder where I am. I'll just text her really quick." She sent the text and hoped her mom wouldn't be mad at him for that too. Given the confrontation at dinner the night before, her mother probably wouldn't be too excited about anything relating to her dad.

"How was school?"

"It was fine. Boring, as usual."

"Are there any fine arts opportunities here? Dance? Theatre?"

She rolled her eyes. "I have no idea. And even if there were, those really aren't interesting to me. I do like shop class, though."

Brandon chuckled under his breath. "Shop class. Exactly what I thought my daughter would like."

"You know, just because I'm female doesn't mean I have to be a girly girl. I like to fish, hike and build things. What's wrong with that?"

Brandon held up his hands. "Nothing wrong with that. Just a surprise. When you were a little girl, you were all about the princess stuff. The pink flowy dresses, the tiaras. Remember that huge dollhouse I built from the kit?"

"Yes, I remember. And the roof caved in about a week after you built it."

Brandon laughed. "I guess you didn't get your ability to build things from me."

"Yeah, I don't know where I got that from. I mean, being around Cooper has helped a lot. He's a contractor. He built that beautiful gazebo and the deck in the back of the house. And he's going to build a treehouse for me. Well, it's more of a platform really…"

"So, you really like Cooper, don't you?"

"Yeah. He's really nice, and he's good to Mom."

There was an awkward moment between them. "It's good that your mother is happy now. Even if she hates me, I'm happy for her."

"Well, maybe you should tell her that."

He shook his head and finished chewing a bite of his sandwich. "I don't think we are meant to have long, deep conversations. Besides, her happiness isn't my concern. I just want to make sure that you're happy."

Evie sat and thought for a moment. "You know what would make me happy?"

"What's that?"

"If all of the adults in my life would stop walking on eggshells and saying rude things to each other. I would just like for everybody to get along, even if they don't like each other. And, I would like for me and you to have some fun while you're here."

He smiled. "Well, then, I'm going to do my best to make all of that happen. I'm sorry for my part in making this whole thing uncomfortable for you. It's just that it's been a long time, and I don't really know where I fit into your life now."

"You're my dad. No one can ever replace you. That's where you fit in."

He smiled and reached across the table to squeeze her hand. For once, Evie felt like maybe things could turn around. Maybe her parents could stop arguing. Maybe she and her dad could connect on some level. At the very least, the fact that he was willing to try made her feel like there might be hope.

TRAVIS STARED at the huge filet mignon in front of him. He wasn't sure if his stomach could fit in that much food. Had it really been this big the last time he ate it?

"Why aren't you eating?" Sam asked. It had taken them about an hour to get a table, but the place was every bit as fancy as he remembered. Sam looked like she fit right in wearing her black blazer and short red skirt. But he was wearing casual khaki pants and a polo shirt, so he definitely didn't look like he was supposed to be there.

"Just admiring the enormous size of this piece of meat. We don't have steaks like this back at home."

"Just think, if you lived here again you could have every kind of food anytime you wanted it. Golden Palace, Indian food, that one Ethiopian place we ate."

Travis laughed. "You seem to forget that I got food poisoning there."

"A minor inconvenience." Sam laughed as she took a sip of her wine.

"I ended up in the emergency room and had to get fluids. I definitely would not consider that a minor inconvenience."

"Okay, so I also brought you here because I wanted to talk to you about something."

"Let me brace myself." He held onto the table in dramatic fashion.

"Oh, stop it! You know I'm your friend, and everything I'm trying to do is to benefit you."

"I know, I know."

"Do you remember my friend Lillian McAfee?

"Lillian McAfee… The name doesn't ring a bell."

"She's the older woman that owns the art gallery. The one who wears the fancy hats and drives that Ferrari with the fuzzy seat covers?"

"Oh, yeah. Right in the heart of Manhattan."

"Correct. Well, anyway, I was talking to Lillian over lunch the other day and your name came up."

"My name came up? What on earth could you have been talking about that would've made my name come up?"

"Fine. I was telling her how I was coming to see you and how excited I was for you. Anyway, I showed her some of your photos from your social media."

"And?"

Sam leaned over the table, a big grin on her face. "Lillian is interested in doing a show featuring your photos."

"What?"

"This could be a huge thing for you. I mean, you'd have to stay in the city for a while, but she's very interested. Plus, she's not just interested in the mountain photos. There are all kinds of other areas and she'd like to make it a long running show of travel photography. You know, we have people from all over the world come to the city and…"

"Sam, stop."

"Why?" she said, looking like she was hurt.

"Look, I appreciate it. I know you're trying to help me, but I don't want help. I don't want to stay in the city. I can't wait to get back home."

"How is that possible? You're so talented, and having a show like this would give you celebrity status. And the money you could make…"

"I don't care about that stuff. Listen, I spent the last decade of my life being miserable. It might not have seemed like it to you, but I was. And then I realized it was because the one person I loved the most in my life wasn't here. And where she goes, I go. The last place I want to be is here in the city without Mia."

Sam sighed and put her head in her hands. "I have to confess something."

"What?"

"All those years that we went to college and then worked together, some of which you were married, I had a huge crush on you."

Travis was shocked. Someone could've knocked him over with a feather. "You did?"

Sam laughed. "Seriously? You couldn't tell? You can't tell right now?"

His eyes widened. "Now?"

"Yes, now. Why do you think I'm fighting so hard to get you to move back? I feel like I missed out on a chance. We would make a great couple."

Travis smiled sadly. "Sam, you're a beautiful woman. You're smart and funny. But there's no way that I'm ever going to be available again. My heart has been somewhere else since I was a teenager."

"But you're going to get stuck in that little town."

He grinned. "I know. And I couldn't be happier about that. I want to marry Mia one day, have a bunch of kids and at least three dogs. I want to paint *our* white picket fence around *our* property. I want to sit on the front porch and drink coffee with her every morning for the rest of my life."

"Don't be offended, but that sounds absolutely dreadful to me," Sam said, laughing.

"You'll find the right person. But, I know it's not me."

"Thank you for being so gracious."

"Of course. I'm flattered."

"I should probably confess something else."

"What's that?"

"Last night, while you were taking your shower, Mia called your phone and I answered it."

Travis's face felt hot. "You did what?"

"I was supposed to tell you that she called, but I just kind of wanted you to myself for a little while."

"Sam! Oh my gosh, she must think something is going on. It took me a couple of hours to call her because we were eating and talking. I bet she thinks the worst."

"I'm so sorry. It was such a juvenile thing to do. But it was my last ditch effort to try to see if I could sway you to come back to the city."

Travis stood up and put his napkin on the table. "I have to go."

"You're not going to eat?"

"No. I need to try to reach Mia and explain. And then I'm going to see if I can find an earlier flight back home."

"Travis, please don't be mad at me…"

He turned back to the table. "I hope you find what you're looking for, Sam." With that, he walked out of the restaurant and headed for the hotel.

CHAPTER 8

*K*ate and Mia stood in the kitchen, staring out into the backyard. "Are you seeing what I'm seeing?"

"Yeah. It's kind of surreal," Mia said.

They were watching Brandon and Evie play football, tossing the ball back and forth over and over. Kate hadn't expected to come home from grocery shopping and find this.

"Maybe they're making progress," Kate said.

"Looks like it. And I'm happy for her. Aren't you?"

Kate smiled. "Actually, I am. Maybe they just needed some time to readjust to each other."

"Hey, y'all," Cooper said, as he walked through the front door. He was holding a large piece of paper with a sketch on it. "Evie around?"

"Oh, just forget that I'm here and ask to see my daughter?" Kate teased. Cooper walked over and kissed her cheek.

"Sorry. I'm just so dang excited about that tree-house. I've got all of the materials out in my truck, and this is the final sketch."

Kate took it from his hand and stared at it. He was so talented and could build anything, and it warmed her heart to see him taking a treehouse for her daughter so seriously.

"What is this part?"

He grinned. "Oh, that's a little overhang in case it rains while she's up there. And look here. That's a built in table so she can put her drink or even a computer."

"You're making it easy for her to live in a tree full-time, Cooper," Mia joked.

"So, where is she?"

"Take a look," Kate said, nodding her head toward the back door. Cooper walked over and saw the football flying through the air.

"Wow. Never thought I'd see that. They actually look like a normal father and daughter for once. Brandon seems out of breath. How long have they been doing this?"

"I'm not sure, but we've been watching for ten minutes," Kate said.

Evie noticed Cooper in the window and waved before putting the football on the ground and jogging over.

"Hey, Cooper. Are you looking for me?"

"I was, but I don't want to interrupt your game. We can chat later."

"Is that the sketch?"

He smiled. "Yep. I'm about to head up and start working."

"Can I go?" she asked, a huge smile on her face.

"You go ahead, sweetie. Old Dad is tired. You wore me out." Brandon was breathing heavily, which was surprising to Kate because he'd always been in good shape.

"Are you sure?"

He squeezed her shoulder. "Of course! Go have fun, and I'll see you tonight at dinner. Besides, I need to make a phone call."

Evie and Cooper walked through the house and out the front door. Mia, sensing she was standing in the middle of an awkward situation, also made herself scarce and disappeared.

Now it was just Kate, standing in front of Brandon, who was still trying to catch his breath.

"Do you want something to drink?" she forced herself to ask.

He looked at her like he was surprised. "Sure. Thanks."

They walked into the kitchen, Brandon pulling the French doors shut behind him. He sat down at the breakfast bar.

"Sweet tea? Water?" Kate said, as she looked in the refrigerator.

"I'll take water. I can't stomach that sweet tea. I'm surprised you can."

She walked over and slid a bottle of water toward

him. "It took me a few months, but I actually prefer it now."

Brandon chuckled. "How? It's like trying to drink sap straight out of the tree."

She couldn't help but laugh at that characterization. "It was nice to see you and Evie enjoying each other again. Kind of reminded me of old times."

"Yeah. She and I used to throw the ball like that all the time when she was a kid. I can't believe how quickly she's grown up."

"It's been tough."

"Has it?" he asked, looking up. They made eye contact for a long moment, Kate struggling not to say something snide or rude. But what was she supposed to say to the father who left his daughter when she needed him most?

"Evie was really struggling back in Rhode Island. She was getting in trouble in school all the time. I thought she would get arrested before too much longer, and then we moved here. She's a whole different kid now."

"Why do you think that is?"

"In Rhode Island, it was just the two of us. She had no roots. No family. Here, she has more than enough family and love to go around. I think it finally filled the hole in her heart that…"

I looked down at his hands. "That I left?"

"Well… Yes."

"Look, Kate, I realize that I went about this reunion the wrong way. I had no right to try to burst into her life and be so confrontational with you. I was just desperate to get some time with her."

"And that's what I don't understand. You've had years to reach out to her and suddenly you need to see her immediately. You were willing to take me to court if you had to. What is that about?"

He cleared his throat, obviously nervous. "I guess I just really felt bad about what I'd done. I wanted to see her before it was too late. I was afraid she would become an adult and never want to see me again."

Kate still wasn't buying it. He was keeping something from her, but if she pushed then she ran the risk of creating more drama.

"Well, I'm happy if she's happy. So, how are Kara and the kids? Certainly they must miss you?"

"They're fine. Kara is modeling swimwear in Cozumel right now. The kids are staying with her parents for a while."

Modeling swimwear? Kate would soon be modeling a beekeeping suit. There was something very wrong with that picture.

"I hope that Evie will get to meet them someday before everybody is much older. She would love to have some siblings."

"You don't think you'll have kids with Cooper?"

"That's a very personal question, but no. That's not in my plan. One kid was plenty."

"For what it's worth, Kate, I'm happy that things are going well for you. You deserve that. And even if I don't understand why the two of you love this place so much, I'm glad you have those roots now that you always wanted."

"Thanks. Well, I think I'm going to head up to the tree and see what my daughter and Cooper are up to. I don't want them building some monstrosity."

"Thanks for the water."

As she walked out of the front door, she thought that maybe she might've misjudged Brandon. Maybe he really had changed and would be a great addition to her daughter's life. But he was still keeping a secret, and until she found out what that was, she wouldn't feel completely comfortable.

MIA HAD FELT that it was best to get out of Dodge when Kate and Brandon were standing in front of her. She figured it was the right time for Kate to have a conversation with her ex-husband, so she went upstairs to her room.

She hadn't heard from Travis since the night before. Of course, then her phone had died after she accidentally dropped it in the dish water. She had it in a bag of rice hoping to get all of the moisture out of it and turn it on again.

If Travis needed anything, it would just have to wait. Or he would call Kate, and she hadn't said anything. The more she thought about it, the more uncomfortable it made her feel that he didn't mention his dinner with Sam. She didn't know a whole lot about their history except that they had gone to college together and worked at the same company for years. Surely if anything was ever going to happen between them, it already would have.

But then again, Travis had been married some of that time. And when his wife passed away, he was in no shape to be dating then either.

Sam seemed like a nice enough person, but her interest in Mia's boyfriend was disconcerting. Maybe they were just friends, or maybe she wanted something more.

Tired of thinking about it, Mia decided that doing laundry was probably a good way to get her mind off of everything. She loaded all of her clothes into a large plastic basket that her mother had always used. One of the handles was cracking, but she couldn't bear to get rid of it. So many Saturday mornings, she remembered her mom walking down the stairs carrying it, overflowing with clothing and towels from the guests.

As she walked down the hall, she noticed that Brandon's door was cracked open. Apparently he and Kate had already finished their conversation. She started to walk but then heard him talking. Curiosity getting the better of her, so she stopped by his door.

"I know. I miss you guys too. Hopefully I won't have to be here much longer…"

Who was he talking to? His wife?

"I haven't said anything yet. But I can't stay here much longer. This place is as boring as it gets…"

Boring? Certainly it wasn't the most exciting

place on earth, but Mia would never classify the beautiful mountains and the stunning lake as boring. Feeling offended, she almost walked away, but she just wanted to hear more.

"I know we're running out of time. I'm going to say something soon. I just don't know if I should say it to Evie or Kate. What do you think?"

Say what? Running out of time? She almost wanted to open the door and ask him what he was talking about, but so far Brandon appeared to be very secretive and probably wouldn't tell her anyway.

"I know I have to. I've been trying to play nicer the last couple of days because you catch more bees with honey. And can you believe my ex is becoming a beekeeper?"

Mia really wanted to walk into the room and dump the dirty laundry right on his head. Why was he playing nice to Kate's face and then saying things like this behind her back?

"One way or another, I'll get what I need. Don't worry, honey…"

It sounded like he was wrapping up his conversation, so Mia quickly walked away and ran down the stairs. She stopped and set the laundry basket on the back of the sofa for a moment. What was he doing? Something is definitely up, just as she and Kate had suspected. But what was it? It sounded like only time would tell how this would play out.

KATE STOOD BESIDE THE TREE, looking up at her daughter and Cooper sitting precariously on a limb. "Are you sure that limb will hold both of you?"

They laughed. "We do this all the time, Mom!" Evie said, rolling her eyes. It was amazing how many times a day a teenager could roll their eyes without falling over backwards.

"Still, I think one of you should come down!" Kate called up to them.

Again, they both laughed. She loved seeing the interaction between Cooper and her daughter. As much as she wanted Evie to have a relationship with Brandon, she also wanted her to feel safe and comfortable around Cooper. After all, one day they might end up married. At least that was her hope, although they'd never really talked about it.

Cooper climbed down out of the tree and gave her a quick peck on her forehead. "I promise I won't let anything break that will send us tumbling to the ground."

"Y'all are crazy, climbing trees like that."

"Did you just say *y'all?*"

Kate laughed. "Apparently this place is rubbing off on me."

"I'm going to back the truck up a little bit more so I can get to the lumber easier."

Cooper walked down the driveway just a bit and hopped into his truck. She turned around to see Evie climbing out of the tree.

"I think me and Dad are really starting to form a bond."

"It certainly looks like it. I'm really happy for you."

"Thanks. Hopefully we can spend a lot more time together, even though he lives in Mexico. I guess that will make it a kind of hard."

Kate froze for a moment. "You're not thinking of moving there with him, are you?"

Evie stared at her and then laughed. "Um, no. I would never leave this place. But maybe he'll invite me for a vacation or something."

"Maybe so. We'll talk about it if that ever happens."

"I would like to meet my brother and sister."

"I know. I'm sure your dad will make that happen at some point soon."

Cooper stopped the truck and popped the tail-gate down. "Hey, Evie, you want to help me start unloading some of this?"

As Kate watched them pull out pieces of lumber, she was so thankful to have found someone like Cooper. Who else would build her daughter a customized treehouse platform just so she could enjoy sitting there? It was going to be a lot of work, and she knew he had other things to do. But he had considered this treehouse project to be just as important as everything he was doing for other people and getting paid.

Kate waited for them to finish unloading some of the lumber and then sat on the tailgate of the truck. She would've helped them, but she had been having problems with her neck lately, probably from stress. The last thing she wanted to do was really pull a muscle and end up not being able to take care of her bees or cook for the guests.

As she watched them start to work, her phone rang. She fished it out of her pocket and didn't recognize the number. "Hello?"

"Kate? It's Sylvia. How are you?"

"I'm good, Sylvia. It's nice to hear from you. We were hoping that you would come to visit with dad."

There was a long pause. "That's why I'm calling you. And I really probably shouldn't be calling you because Jack would kill me, but I have to tell you girls something. I've actually driven into town, but he doesn't know that I'm here. I hope we can keep this between us until I have a chance to meet with you girls."

"Meet with us? Is everything okay?"

As Kate continued listening to Sylvia, she noticed Mia walking up the driveway.

"What's going on?"

Kate held up her hand. "So where would you like to meet us, Sylvia?"

"*Sylvia?*" Mia mouthed.

"The café? Oh, you mean the one in Blue Falls?"

"*She wants us to come two cities over?*"

"Okay. We will see you in a bit."

Kate ended the call and looked at her sister, her mouth hanging open a bit.

"What's going on?"

"That was Sylvia, and she said that she has something she needs to talk to us about but she doesn't want Dad to know she's driven to town to meet with us. We have to meet her away from here, just so we don't run into him."

"Well, I don't like the sound of that."

"Neither do I, and I don't like keeping anything from him. But we know he's keeping a secret, and I think we need to meet her."

"Speaking of secrets…"

"Is everything okay?" Cooper called down. Not wanting to upset her daughter, Kate decided to keep her conversation with Sylvia to herself.

"Everything is fine. But Mia and I have an errand we need to run, so will be back in a couple of hours."

"Okay. Love you!" Cooper called.

She smiled at him. "Love you too! And don't fall out of the tree!"

"Y'all are so sweet."

"So are you and Travis."

"Don't even get me started about that…"

"Obviously we need to talk about whatever that is, but right now I think we need to focus on getting to Sylvia and finding out exactly what's going on with Dad. Wait, were you going to tell me something else?"

Mia paused for a moment. "No. It can wait."

The two of them jogged down the driveway, climbed into Kate's car and took off in pursuit of answers about what was going on with their father.

～

KATE AND MIA parked the car and hurried into the cafe. The drive over had done nothing for either of their worried minds. In the car, they'd talked about their dad, Mia's worries with Travis and Cooper building the treehouse, but Mia had kept Brandon's overheard conversation a secret for now. She didn't want to add any more worries to Kate's already full plate.

"It looks like she's here," Kate said, as they pulled up at the café. They could see Sylvia sitting inside, and she raised a hand to wave at them.

They walked into the café, the smell of food overwhelming Mia's senses. She was starving and thankful to get away from the B&B for a while where someone else was cooking for her.

"Sylvia, it's so good to see you," Kate said, smiling as she hugged Sylvia tightly. Mia hugged her as well before they both sat down. Sylvia looked tired, worried.

"I'm so thankful that you two agreed to meet me here. And you didn't tell your father, right?"

"We didn't. We don't feel great about it, but we know he's hiding something and we've been worried about it," Mia said.

"Welcome to Della's Cafe," the young female server said as she walked up to the table. "Can I get you something to drink?"

"Sweet tea for both of us," Mia said, forcing a smile. Her mother had always taught her to be kind and mannerly even when things were a mess in her mind.

As the waitress walked away, Sylvia sucked in a deep breath and slowly blew it out like she was preparing for something really bad. Mia's stomach tightened.

"You're right that your father has been keeping something from you."

"Are you two having marriage trouble?" Kate asked.

Sylvia smiled slightly and shook her head. "No. I mean, the fact that he is keeping this secret from y'all has caused us a few fights recently, but that's not it."

"What is it?"

"Your father has a health problem that is very serious. His doctors want him to have a procedure, and he's refusing. He told me he's just going to let nature take it's course, and I think he's just scared."

"But he seems fine. What kind of health problem?" Kate asked, confused.

"A few weeks ago, he had a cough. We didn't really think anything of it because we figured it was a cold or something like that. Then he woke up one morning and he couldn't breathe well, so I ended up taking him to the emergency room. I wanted to call you girls, but he wouldn't allow it."

"He's a stubborn old goat," Mia said, rolling her eyes.

"Yes, he is," Sylvia said, smiling sadly. "Long story short, they found out that he has the beginnings of congestive heart failure."

"Oh my gosh!" Kate said, putting her hand over her mouth.

"Thankfully, the doctors were able to treat a lot of the issues in the hospital. They released him and he's been taking medication ever since, but they sent him to see a cardiologist."

"And what did they say?"

"The doctor said that he has a potentially dangerous heart rhythm. There were two options that they gave us. One would be to have a procedure called an ablation. They would basically burn the part of his heart that is causing the arrhythmia. That might save his heart function and keep the heart failure from progressing."

"Wow. That sounds really scary and possibly dangerous." Mia said.

"Actually, it's apparently a very common procedure. He probably wouldn't even stay overnight at the hospital."

"You said there was another option?" Kate asked.

"The other option would be to get a defibrillator implanted in his chest. If his heart goes into a potentially fatal arrhythmia, it would shock his heart."

Mia's eyes widened and her mouth dropped open. "That sounds terrible. So he would be walking around like a ticking time bomb?"

"Exactly. And something like that really wouldn't help add more years to his life. The doctor definitely wants him to have the ablation first. Sometimes they can't identify the area of the heart that's causing the problem, and they may have to even repeat the ablation. Sometimes they do the procedure and it causes a worse problem to happen."

Kate put her head in her hands. "This is all very scary. We just got him in our lives, and now something like this?"

"I know. And I begged him to tell you girls. I begged him over and over, but he just wouldn't listen. He said he wanted to come spend time with you because he's convinced maybe he doesn't have much time left."

"Is that what the doctor is saying?" Mia asked, her eyes filling with tears.

"Not in so many words, but it's not a good prognosis if he just doesn't do anything. His heart function will decrease if he doesn't address the arrhythmia. I think the ablation is our best chance. It's the least invasive."

"So you want us to talk to him?"

"I just thought maybe you girls would be able to talk some sense into him. Doing nothing is just not a reasonable way to go about this."

"We have to make him get the procedure. I can't lose my dad after I just found him," Kate said, a tear rolling down her cheek. Mia hated to see her strong sister so upset, even though she was feeling the same way.

"We will talk to him, and we will make him understand that he has to do this. I'm sure he's just really scared, and that's totally understandable."

"He told me that he was afraid of having the procedure because what if he died and never saw you two again? At least if he does nothing, he knows he'll have that time with you, or at least that's the way he's thinking about it."

"We're going to change his mind," Kate said, wiping away her tears. "We just have to."

CHAPTER 9

*T*ravis stood at the airport desk and ran his fingers through his hair. The stress was going to kill him. He'd tried calling Mia for hours, and she wasn't answering. Since it was going straight to voicemail, he could only assume that she was ignoring his calls. What Sam had done was inexcusable, and he could only hope Mia trusted him.

"Please, there's got to be something," he said again.

"I'm so sorry, sir, but the next flight is booked solid. Your ticket for tomorrow morning is going to be your best bet," the ticket agent said.

"What about stand-by?"

"You can wait here and see if anything opens up on the next flight in a couple of hours, but it's usually pretty booked."

"Okay, thanks. I'll be waiting right over here. Please let me know."

He walked back to his seat and sat down, determined to get home as soon as possible. Getting back tomorrow wouldn't be terrible, but it was killing him to think that Mia called him and Sam answered. And he was in the shower, of all things. What must she be thinking?

Still, she hadn't said anything when they spoke after that. Why? Had it just not bothered her? Maybe she didn't think anything of it. But why wasn't she answering her phone?

Then it dawned on him that something could be wrong. What if she was hurt? He pulled his phone out of his pocket and dialed Kate's number. It rang several times and went to voicemail. He hung up and called Cooper.

"Hello?"

"Thank God someone around there is answering the dang phone!"

"Who is this?"

Travis could hear birds in the background. "It's Travis. And why do I hear birds?"

"I'm up in a tree. What's up?"

"Why are you up in a... You know what, never mind. Do you know where Mia is?"

"She walked up the driveway a little while ago, and she took off with Kate."

"So she's okay?"

"Yeah. Why wouldn't she be?"

"She hasn't been answering my calls. I thought something might be wrong."

"Oh. Well, she seems fine. Although..."

"Although what?"

"I did notice that she and Kate were talking about something, and they both looked worried or upset. Not sure what that was about."

"Oh no."

"What's going on?"

"Nothing. Listen, if you see her, please ask her to call me, okay?"

"Will do."

Travis ended the call and leaned his head back, staring up at the ceiling. He'd waited most of his life to be with Mia again, and he wasn't going to let a silly misunderstanding get in the way of their happily ever after.

KATE PULLED into the driveway at a rapid clip. "Slow down before you kill the two of us!" Mia said, holding onto the dashboard. Kate had always been a speedy driver, a fact that worried her when it came to teaching Evie to drive. Now, she'd have to teach her on curvy mountain roads which would certainly be an adventure.

"Sorry. I'm just so stressed out. I can't believe that Dad is going into heart failure and doesn't want to do anything about it."

She stopped the car and sat there for a moment, her hands gripping the steering wheel. She took a deep breath and blew it out.

"We need to find Dad and have a talk with him as soon as possible."

"I agree, but we should think about how we're going to approach this. I don't want to stress him out any further," Kate said.

"You're right. We have to be careful."

They got out of the car and walked into the house. Evie was fixing herself a snack, which would probably ruin her dinner later, and Brandon was sitting at the breakfast bar watching her.

"How'd the treehouse building go?" Mia asked, trying to sound nonchalant.

"Cooper is still up there. I needed a snack."

"I hope you offered to make him one too," Kate said, pointing her finger.

"I did but he had something with him. Me and Dad were going to go down and do a little fishing before dinner."

"Is that okay with you, Kate?" Brandon asked.

The room suddenly fell silent for a moment. "That's fine. Thank you for asking."

Inside, Mia seethed. She hadn't told her sister about the phone call she overheard with Brandon, and now it was very apparent that he was just trying to play nice. What was his end goal?

Right now, she couldn't think about it. She was so worried about her own father that everything else had to take a back seat, including worrying about Travis. That was such a minor thought at the moment. Her petty relationship worries could be thought about later.

"Have you seen your grandpa around?" Mia asked.

"Not lately. Maybe he's in his room?"

"Okay, I'll check there." Mia trotted up the stairs and looked for her father but didn't see him anywhere. She peered out the window and noticed he was sitting down on the dock. Talking to him right now wasn't going to work if Evie and Brandon were going to be down there fishing.

Mia came back down the stairs and pulled Kate aside. "He's not up there. He's on the dock."

"I guess we're going to have to wait a little while before we talk to him. Maybe we can lure him back to the house with cut up hotdogs?" Kate joked.

Having to wait longer to talk to their dad was going to be anxiety producing, but one way or the another they were going to talk to him before the day was at an end.

EVIE SAT on the edge of the dock, her fishing line in the water. They weren't biting today, but she was enjoying the time she was getting to spend with her father.

Surprisingly, he hadn't mentioned yet when he planned to leave. He'd been there almost a week now, and she assumed he needed to go back home at some point. He seemed to be settling in quite well, and it made her wonder if maybe he wasn't happy back in Mexico. Maybe he would move there to be closer to her.

Over the last couple of days, she had allowed

herself to hope. To dream. To see herself in a future that included her father.

She thought about how wonderful birthdays might be, especially if she got to know her sister and brother. She thought she would make a good older sibling, always protecting and guiding them. She wanted to show them how *not* to get in trouble like she had when she was back in Rhode Island.

She thought about Thanksgiving and Christmas. If her parents could continue to get along, maybe they could all be one big, happy family, sitting around the table, telling jokes and stories. Sure, it was probably like one of those cheesy holiday movies you see on TV, but maybe it could be real life.

"We sure aren't having any luck, are we?" Brandon said.

"Nope. Sometimes, that's how it happens. I guess that's why grandpa stopped fishing for the day. Maybe he scared them all away," she said, laughing.

Brandon pulled his line in and set his fishing pole beside him. He seemed a little nervous all of the sudden, but she didn't know why. They'd been having a nice conversation about his life back in Mexico and how he had tried all kinds of new foods over the years that he wanted Evie to get a chance to try. He regaled her with stories of Carmelita, a local woman who made the best enchiladas he'd ever had.

She brought up the idea of going there on vacation at some point, and he seemed to be receptive to it, although he didn't commit.

"I really enjoy going out in the canoe and kayak sometimes. I don't usually fish that way, but it's really relaxing when you…"

"Evie, we need to talk."

"Okay…" She reeled in her line and put her pole behind her. "What's going on?"

He reached over and held her hand. "You know that I love you, right?"

"Of course. And I love you too."

"I need to ask you something, and it's a big deal. In fact, it's a life or death deal."

"What are you talking about, Dad?"

"I don't know quite how to say this. So I'm just going to say it and get it out because I've been keeping this in for a long time."

"You're scaring me."

He looked at her in a way she had never seen, his face almost sad, his eyes looking directly into hers. "Honey, I'm dying."

Evie felt like she couldn't breathe. She pulled her hand away and put it up to her chest. Her heart rate quickened, and she could feel her face starting to flush. She had never passed out in her life, but she assumed this is what people felt like right before they hit the ground.

"You're dying? That can't be right. I don't understand!"

"Take a breath. Just calm down," he said, trying to get her to focus.

"But you just reconnected with me. You can't be dying…"

"I was diagnosed a year ago with a rare blood disorder. If I don't do the treatment, I won't make it another year, maybe two."

She felt the tears stinging her eyes and then overflowing down her face. "Then do the treatment! You have to do the treatment!"

"Honey, it's not that simple. It's a special kind of treatment."

"What do you mean? If there's a treatment, you have to do it. You can't just leave me, or my brother and sister!"

"Trust me, I don't want to leave any of you. But so far, there have been no matches."

"Matches? What do you mean?"

"You see, sweetie, I need a bone marrow transplant. And that's one of the reasons that I'm here. My wife, and your brother and sister, they're not matches. I'm here because I'm hoping that you'd be willing to get tested over at the hospital and see if you're a match for me."

Suddenly, she was overflowing with emotion. Had her father only come back because he wanted her bone marrow? Had he really ever had any interest in having a relationship with her, or was this all about saving his own life?

At the same time, she wanted to save him. She wanted to do anything she could to keep him alive. The conflicting emotions felt like a tornado inside of her gut.

"Did you talk to Mom about this?"

"No. Maybe I should have, but I wanted to talk to

you first. I didn't want anyone making the decision for you."

"What does this procedure entail?"

"It's a very simple procedure, from what I understand. You might be in the hospital for most of the day, maybe overnight. But if you're a match, you'll save my life."

Evie stood up. Brandon looked up at her, confused.

"I need some time to think. I… I can't do this right now…" She turned and ran toward the house, leaving her father sitting on the dock, calling out to her.

Right now, she needed to be alone and think about what her father had just told her. It was a lot to take in, and the pressure was just too much.

"THERE YOU ARE," Kate said as she and Mia walked into the backyard. They'd spent the last hour talking about how to approach their father. Now, as Kate stood in front of him in the gazebo, she felt ill-equipped.

"I didn't know you were looking for me. Am I in trouble?" he asked with a smile.

"Maybe," Mia muttered under her breath.

They sat down across from him at the picnic table. "What are you doing out here?"

"Reminiscing."

"Reminiscing about what?" Mia asked. It was odd

that he was just sitting there staring off into the distance.

"To be honest? I'm thinking about your momma."

"About Momma? What do you mean?"

"Well, when I come to the B&B, I can feel her presence. It gives me peace."

"I know what you mean. Momma is all over this place. I can feel her everywhere," Mia said, the grief she tried to keep tamped down coming to the surface yet again.

"I remember when we'd hike these trails as teenagers. She was so young and outgoing, and I felt completely inadequate in the shadow of her. I wondered how anyone like her could be interested in a tall, gangly guy like me."

"Dad, we know." Kate blurted it out so quickly that even Mia was surprised.

"Know what?"

"Sylvia called," Mia said softly.

They watched him process the information for a moment. His jaw tightened. His face hardened. "She had no right to do that."

"She's your wife, and she's worried about you. We're all worried about you," Kate said, reaching for his hand.

"This is my decision, and she's been pressuring me."

"Dad, she wants what's best for you. This is a serious situation."

"Do you think I don't know that? Look, I know you girls want to talk about this, but I really don't."

Jack stood up and started to walk toward the house.

"You have to get the ablation," Kate said loudly.

Jack turned around. "I don't have to do anything. And I'm not going to. Look, God has a plan for all of us, and this is just His plan for me."

"That's a crock and you know it!" Mia said. Kate was surprised that her little sister had spoken up so strongly.

"Excuse me?"

"You're scared, Dad. We get it. But, maybe God is giving you the gift of options. Did you ever think about that?"

"I don't like either option," he said, turning to walk again.

"Do you know who would've loved options? My momma! And she'd be so mad at you right now!"

Jack turned again. "Mad at me? Why?"

"Because you're our last living parent, and we just got you in our lives. You're supposed to take care of us until God calls you home, and you're giving up! She'd smack you right across your cheek and bless you out if she was here."

Kate loved this side of Mia. She'd never seen it before, but it was certainly effective. Jack paused for a long moment and then walked back to the picnic table, sitting down.

"I love you girls. You know that. But this procedure isn't a sure thing. They might not be able to find the spot causing the arrhythmia, and then what? More procedures?"

"I watched Momma fight until there were no other options. That's what you do to stay with the ones you love," Mia said, a tear rolling down her cheek. Jack reached over and grabbed each of their hands.

"We'll be here for you, Dad. No matter what. Just please don't give up," Kate said.

"I'll tell you what. I'll get a second opinion at a hospital in Atlanta. If that doctor agrees, I'll get the ablation. Okay?"

Kate was so relieved. "Thank you!"

The girls rushed over and hugged Jack tightly. There was hope again, and for that, Kate was beyond grateful.

COOPER SAT on the tailgate of his truck, needing a break after so many hours of working on the tree-house platform. He wanted to get it done to see Evie's face when it was finished. But he also had other work to do around town on various projects, so he knew he couldn't take up too much time building it. It wasn't that complicated of a structure, so he thought he would have it finished within the next day or so.

When he saw Evie walking up the driveway, he was surprised. She was supposed to be spending time with her father. He was concerned when he saw the look on her face. She looked like she'd been crying.

"Hey. What's the matter? You look really upset."

Evie walked over and sat down next to him on the tailgate. "My dad told me that he's dying."

"What?"

"We were fishing, and he told me that he has some kind of rare blood disease and he needs me to donate my bone marrow."

Cooper felt anger well up within him. Who told a kid something like that? Kate hadn't mentioned it, which probably meant the Brandon hadn't talked to her first.

"Evie, have you talked to your mom about this?"

"No. And I'm not going to right now."

"You have to. This is way too big for someone your age to handle."

"Cooper, you have to promise me you won't tell her. I just want to be able to think about it on my own for a while. Maybe I'll tell her tomorrow."

"I'll give you until lunchtime tomorrow. At that point, you have to promise me that you'll talk to your mom."

"Okay, fine."

He looked at her, and it pained him to see the sadness on her face. "I'm sure your dad will be fine."

"Honestly, I'm not even thinking about that right now. I'm wondering… Well, I'm honestly wondering if he only came here because he needs me for something. Would he have ever reached out if he didn't need my bone marrow?"

It was a good question. A valid one. And Cooper didn't want to say what he really thought. The odds were that Brandon never would've reached out to his daughter if he didn't need something from her. Right now, he wanted to go push him in the lake.

"He's your dad, and I know he loves you. I've seen it in his face, like when y'all were throwing the football."

"I don't know. I get the feeling that he's only here because there's something in it for him. I had really hoped he came here just because he wanted to see me, just because he loved me. But I don't think that's true."

"So what do you think you want to do?"

"I don't know. He's my dad, and even if he's doing this for all the wrong reasons, I don't think I could live with myself if I didn't donate and he died."

"You don't even know if you're a match yet. Don't put that kind of pressure on yourself, Evie."

"Do you mind if I just sit out here with you for a while?"

Cooper put his arm around her. "Sure. You can sit with me for as long as you need."

She laid her head on his shoulder, and he could hear her crying softly. And they sat that way until the sun started to go down, Cooper supporting this girl that he already thought of as his own daughter.

CHAPTER 10

M ia laid on her bed, staring at the ceiling. Travis was supposed to be home tomorrow, and she couldn't wait to see him. It had been a stressful few days, and not having him to lean on had made it all the worse.

Everyone had skipped dinner and opted to eat on their own. Evie seemed upset about something and had stayed up at the tree with Cooper until it was dark. Brandon had never come out of his room. Jack had gone to town to have dinner with Sylvia and mend fences. And Kate had eventually gone to eat at Cooper's house.

That left Mia alone, sitting in her room with a leftover ham sandwich and a heart that missed Travis. She hadn't heard from him since the day before because her phone had gotten wet. Unfortunately, the rice hadn't fixed the moisture issue and she would have to replace the phone.

She looked up at the ceiling and wondered what

her mother would think about the way she handled her father. She had to say that she was pretty impressed with her ability to think on her feet. Sometimes guilt was a powerful motivator, and she didn't care if that's what it took to get her father to fight for his life.

Just as she was about to get up and put on her nightgown, she heard something hit her window. It was a little jolting since nobody ever came down their driveway this late at night. Surely, it was just a little bug or something hitting the glass.

Bang!

There is was again. What was that?

She stood up and crept over to the window, being careful not to let anyone on the other side see her. She peeked out of the side of the curtain and couldn't believe what she saw. Travis!

He was standing there, a bouquet of roses in one hand and a rock in the other.

"Travis? What on Earth are you doing?" she said, laughing, as she opened the window. "I thought you weren't coming home until tomorrow?"

"I wasn't, but I took an earlier flight. I need to talk to you."

"Okay. I'm coming down."

She quickly ran down the stairs and out the front door to find Travis waiting at the bottom of the stairs. She ran straight into his arms, almost knocking the bouquet out of his hand.

"I missed you so much!" she said, burying her face in his chest.

"I missed you too," he said, kissing the top of her head. "But, I have to say that I'm surprised at this reaction."

Mia pulled back. "What? Why?"

He sat down on the step and pulled her down with him. "I know what Sam did."

"What did Sam do?"

"You called when I was in the shower…"

"Oh. That."

"I'm so sorry, Mia."

Suddenly, her stomach tightened. Why was he sorry? What had he done to be sorry for?

"Sorry? So you and Sam…"

Travis looked shocked. "No! Of course not! I meant that I'm sorry she didn't tell me you called. I had no idea until earlier today. That's why I took the first flight home. I sat at the airport on stand-by all day."

"You did?"

"And when you wouldn't answer my calls…"

"Sorry. My phone fell in the water and died. I need a new one."

Travis chuckled. "Yes, you do. I thought all day long that you were mad at me. I fully expected for you to throw eggs at me when I got here tonight."

"Why didn't you call Kate?"

"I did. She never answered. And I called Cooper. Did he not tell you?"

"Cooper has been in a tree all day. I haven't seen him."

"Wow. A bunch of miscommunication, huh?"

"Seems that way. So, tell me about Sam. Why did she do that?"

Travis sighed. "I never knew Sam had feelings for me."

"I could've told you that, Travis. I saw the way she looked at you."

"Why didn't you tell me then?" he asked, with a laugh.

"Because I didn't want you to think that I was jealous, even though I was."

Travis ran his thumb across her cheek. "Mia, you should never be jealous of anyone. I've spent most of my adult life missing you, and there's no way any woman would be able to pull me away from you."

She leaned in and kissed him. "How'd the meeting go?"

"Great. I got the contract!"

"Congratulations, Travis! I'm so proud of you."

"And that means the world to me," he said, pulling her into an embrace and making everything in the world perfect again.

KATE WAS EXHAUSTED. After the conversation she and Mia had had with their father the day before, she'd had a fitful sleep. All she really wanted to do was lay down and nap for the rest of the day, but instead she was standing with Darrell, wearing a beekeeping suit, and looking at her new hives.

"Did you know a single bee will only produce

about one-twelfth of a teaspoon of honey in its life-time?" Darrell was all bees, all the time. He loved what he did, and Kate admired him for that.

"I did not know that," she said, struggling to keep her eyes open.

"Now, one hive can make sixty to one hundred pounds of honey a year…"

He kept talking and talking and talking. Kate tried to pay close attention, but she felt like curling up in the bee suit might actually be more comfortable.

"The queen bee goes on a mating flight once in her lifetime. She leaves the hive and mates with anywhere from five to forty-five drones and then stores the sperm."

"Sounds like the queen gets around a little too much…" Kate mumbled.

"What was that?"

"Oh, nothing."

"Mom?" Evie was standing on the other side of the gazebo, too scared to come very close to the bees. She had been stung once as a small child, and she was definitely not a fan.

"Oh, hey, honey. Did you need something?"

"I was hoping we could talk for a minute?"

Kate turned back to Darrell. "Can you excuse me for a few minutes? I need to go talk to my daughter."

"Of course. Take all the time you need. I'll just be over here communing with the bees," he said, holding his hands out like he was about to direct an orchestra. What an odd little man he was.

Kate walked over to the deck where Evie was sitting, her hands in her lap, nervously fidgeting.

She sat down across from her. "Is everything okay? You look like you're upset about something."

"I don't know quite how to talk about this."

"Is this about your dad? I haven't seen him today."

"I don't know where he is, actually. But, it is about dad."

Kate knew it. Something had been up with him since the day he arrived, and it looked like her daughter had figured out what it was. Or maybe something else had happened that she wasn't aware of.

"What's going on?"

"Dad is dying." Evie spit the words out like she'd been holding them in and was drowning on them.

"What?"

"He told me yesterday. He has a rare blood disorder and they've given him one or maybe two years left to live. That's why he seems so out of breath all the time."

Kate reached across and held her daughter's hand. "I'm so sorry to hear that, Evie. I know that had to be really tough for your dad to tell you that. So he wanted to come here and spend time with you because he doesn't have much time left?"

She shook her head. "No. I mean, maybe that's part of it, but it's not the main reason."

"What do you mean?"

"He came here because he needs a bone marrow match, and he was hoping that would be me."

Kate had never felt such anger well up within her. It felt like it was going to overwhelm her body and blow off the top of her head. She couldn't believe what she was hearing. How could any father go straight to his teenage daughter and ask her for bone marrow without talking to her mother first?

And how could a father who hadn't seen his daughter in years come back and make such a big request?

"You've got to be kidding me!"

"Look, I knew you would be upset which is why I didn't tell you yesterday. I needed some time to think about what I wanted to do."

"What do you want to do? You're a kid! You have no business making a decision like this, Evie. That wasn't fair for your father to put you on the spot like that."

"He's my dad. And I will be an adult in a couple of years. I think I should have some input in this, Mom."

Kate took a deep breath and then blew it out slowly. She knew that she needed to calm down, if for no other reason than to not alienate her daughter. Evie was right. She should have input as to whether to get tested.

"You're right. I'm sorry. And now that you've had some time to think, what are you thinking?"

"I'm thinking that it's the right thing to do. If he died and I had any chance of saving him, I would never forgive myself."

Kate could understand that. After all, if her father

needed something like that from her, she would move heaven and earth to do it even if they didn't have a good relationship.

"Have you spoken to him today?"

"No. I don't even know where he is."

"I think we should talk about this as a family, don't you?"

She nodded. "I think so."

"Why don't you go hang out with Cooper? I think he is almost finished with your treehouse. I'll find your dad, and we will set up a time to talk as a family. Sound good?"

"Okay." She stood up and hugged her mother, something that she rarely did. "Thanks for being there."

"Always."

As she watched Evie walk around the house and then up the driveway, she felt a mix of emotions. Pride in her daughter, and plenty of anger towards her ex-husband. Now, she had to find him.

KATE HAD DRIVEN ALL over town looking for her ex-husband. He was nowhere to be found. When she got back to the B&B, she waved at Cooper and Evie, who were now sitting on the tree platform. Mia was welcoming a new family that had come to stay at the B&B, and Travis was apparently taking pictures to use for the new book.

Still, she didn't see Brandon. He wasn't by the

lake, in the gazebo or on the deck. Had he left town without saying goodbye?

"Mia, have you seen Brandon?" she asked when she walked in the door. Mia shook her head.

"Not at all today."

"I don't know where he is. It's strange. Did he come down this morning?"

At that moment, Mia and Kate stared at each other. Was Brandon still in his room after lunchtime? Kate ran up the stairs as fast as she could, worried about what she'd find. She opened the door to Brandon's room and he was laying in the bed, the cover pulled around his neck, his complexion pale.

"Brandon? Are you okay?" She immediately ran over to his bedside and felt his forehead. He was burning up.

"I'm cold," he said, his voice shaking.

"What happened?" Mia asked from the doorway.

"I need you to call the paramedics. And call Cooper to bring Evie home. Quick!"

The next twenty minutes were a blur. Evie running in and seeing her dad, tears starting to stream down her face. Cooper holding Kate in his arms while she watched the paramedics load Brandon onto a stretcher. Everything seemed to be going in slow motion.

Cooper agreed to watch the B&B while Mia, Kate and Evie followed the ambulance to the hospital. Evie cried the whole way, worried that it was too late to save her dad.

As they sat in the waiting room, Kate realized all

of her anger at Brandon was gone. He was so sick. She wasn't sure he'd make it out of this alive, and she almost felt guilty for the way she was thinking about him hours earlier. Of course, he shouldn't have asked Evie without her knowledge, but now she realized how desperate he must've been. He probably thought Kate would have said no, and he couldn't take the risk.

"Do you think he's going to die?" Evie asked softly.

"I don't know, honey. I wish I knew what was going on back there."

"Did anybody call Kara?" Mia asked.

"I don't even have her number. Maybe you can look her up on social media? See if you can reach her?" Kate said.

"Good idea. I'll go outside and see if I can get better cell service."

Mia walked out of the emergency room and left Kate alone with her daughter. She didn't really know what to say to make it better. Brandon had appeared to be in bad shape when he was loaded into the ambulance. Kate couldn't help but think back to the time when they were actually in love with each other, when he was her world. She didn't understand what had happened to him over the years to make him leave his daughter behind like that, but she still had enough love tucked away in the deep recesses of her heart to want him to survive this.

"Are you Brandon's wife?" a nurse came out and asked. For a moment, she almost said "ex", but then she realized they wouldn't let her back there if she did. Certainly, a little white lie wouldn't hurt. He needed someone to advocate for him right now.

"Yes. And this is his daughter, Evie."

"Follow me."

They went through some automated glass doors and through a bunch of triage rooms before the nurse led them into a small office. This wasn't good. The small rooms were usually where bad news was presented, giving the people receiving that news somewhere to grieve and cry in private.

"The doctor will be in shortly," the nurse said, before shutting the door.

"Do you think he died?" Evie asked, suddenly panic-stricken.

"We don't know anything yet, Ev. Don't assume the worst, okay?" She rubbed her arm and prayed that Brandon was still alive. Losing him now would crush her daughter and always make her wonder if she could've saved him somehow.

"Sorry to keep you folks waiting," the doctor said. He was an extremely tall man with brown hair and glasses, and he towered above them until he sat down on a rolling chair in front of them.

"How's my dad?"

He looked at her with a compassionate expression, and Kate braced herself for the worst. "He's stable right now."

"Is that good?" Evie asked, hopeful.

"Your father has a blood disease."

"Like a cancer?"

"Yes, like that. It's quite advanced. Had he explained this to you?"

"He only told us yesterday. We've been... apart... for years. He came to visit Evie and told her."

He looked at them like he was confused at their family dynamic, but thankfully kept talking. "Without a bone marrow transplant, he doesn't have long to live."

"His doctors back home said one or two years," Evie said.

"I'm afraid this latest setback doesn't point in that direction. I would say a few weeks if something isn't done."

"Weeks? Oh my gosh!" Evie said, tears pouring down her cheeks.

"I understand he's on the bone marrow registry, but they haven't found a match yet..."

"I want to be tested."

"You would need parental permission..."

"She has my permission," Kate said, quickly. "And I'd like to be tested as well. And I'm sure my sister would too."

The doctor smiled. "This man must be well loved by your family."

Kate cleared her throat. "So, how do we get tested?"

"THIS WAIT IS UNBEARABLE," Kate said, sitting at the breakfast bar. She, Mia and Evie had all been tested

145

earlier in the week, and the results were supposed to be ready by now. Every moment of the day, she and Evie stared at their phones. That had resulted in Evie failing a test because she was so distracted at school.

Brandon was still in the hospital, although he was doing better and remaining stable. Evie visited him everyday after school and a couple of times on the weekends. They would play card games, watch silly videos and talk about old times. Kate had gone once or twice, and they'd been able to talk through some things too.

While she would never understand why Brandon left their daughter the way he did, she couldn't let that fester in her heart any longer. She had to let it go because Evie seemed to have let it go.

"You know, Momma always said a watched pot never boils," Mia said as she wiped down the counter after cooking breakfast.

"You realize that doesn't make sense, right? If you put water on a hot stove, it will boil no matter how long you watch it," Kate said, monotone.

"You ruin everything," Mia said, laughing. "Either way, watching your phone isn't going to make it ring any faster."

As if on cue, Kate's phone vibrated across the countertop. "I guess you're wrong," she said, smiling. "Hello? Yes, this is she. Really? Okay. We will head that way."

"Was that the hospital?"

"Yes. They have the results and want us to come as soon as we can."

"Should we check Evie out of school?"

"Absolutely. Let's go!"

Thirty minutes later, they had picked up Evie and were pulling into the hospital parking lot. Kate's stomach was so nervous that it felt like drunk pigeons were fighting over a piece of bread in there.

The nurse took them back to Brandon's room. He was watching some court show on TV. The case seemed to be about two friends who'd rented an apartment together, but one of them bailed on rent. It seemed like the most boring show she'd ever watched, yet Kate kept listening to it in the background while they waited for the doctor.

"How're you feeling today, Dad?" Evie asked, as she walked over and hugged him.

Today, Brandon was sitting up eating pudding and his color looked better. But the doctor had warned them privately that his condition had not improved, only the medications were masking it enough to give him a little more time.

"Good. How was school?"

"Same old, same old."

"And how are you, Kate?" he asked, a genuine smile on his face.

"I'm good. I hear Kara is coming tomorrow?"

"Yes. She's bringing the kids too. I can't wait for Evie to meet them."

"I'm so excited to be a big sister!"

"Hey, folks. I'm glad you could get here so quickly," Dr. Ames said. As tall as Kate was, he seemed ten feet taller.

"We're anxious to get these results," Kate said.

"Well, then, let's not delay." He had three envelopes in his hands, and they appeared to be unopened. "I figured it was best to just do this here together. First up, we have Mia." He ripped open the envelope and read the paper inside. "Mia, you are not a match."

"No big surprise there," she said, shrugging her shoulders. "I mean, we're not related."

"Actually, you don't have to be related to be a match. Often, family members aren't a match, believe it or not."

That made Kate squirm. Surely, Evie would be a match and this nightmare would be over.

"Okay, now we have Evie." He ripped open that envelope and his face fell a bit. "I'm sorry."

"Wait, what? I'm not a match? That can't be possible! I'm his daughter!" Evie said, her eyes welling up.

"It happens. I'm really sorry."

"Honey, it's okay," Brandon said, reaching for her hand.

"No, it's not. You came here because you thought I could save you, and I can't."

"I didn't come here just because of that, Evie. I love you, and this time together has been the best medicine for me."

Kate's heart warmed a bit. Maybe he'd come there under some false pretenses, but it had all worked out in the end. At least somewhat.

"Last one I have here is for Kate…"

"*I'm not a match,*" she said, under her breath.

"Congratulations, Brandon! You have a match!"

Kate and Brandon locked eyes. "What?" she said.

"You are a great match for Brandon."

"I am?"

"Oh my gosh, Mom! You can save Dad!"

Kate felt her heart beating in her head. That wasn't a good sign, right? How was this possible? She was his match?

"I'm going to give you folks some time together. The nurse will come in later to talk about the transplant procedures."

As the doctor left, all eyes turned to Kate.

"What a blessing!" Mia said, smiling. Evie was drowning in happy tears as she hugged Brandon. But he was looking at Kate.

"Kate? You okay?" he finally said.

"I'm just in shock…"

"Evie and Mia, can I talk to Kate alone for a minute?"

They nodded and left the room, pulling the sliding glass door closed. Kate stood across the room feeling frozen to the floor for some reason.

"Sit," he said, pointing to the chair next to him.

She walked over and sat down, her face still stuck in some kind of surprised expression.

"Kate, I know that we have some history, so if you don't want to do this…"

She turned her head quickly and looked at him. "You're kidding me, right? First of all, my daughter would never forgive me if I didn't do this. Second of all, I would never let another human being die if there was something I could do to save them."

"Still, this is a surgical procedure, and there might be some risk involved…"

"Brandon, I appreciate what you're saying but I'm going to do this. The best gift that I can give my daughter is to finally have her father in her life again. But you have to promise me something."

"Okay. What's that?"

"You know, before I found you sick in your bed, I was trying to find you so that I could yell at you for asking Evie to donate bone marrow. I was so fuming mad at you."

"Understandable. I realize it was the wrong thing to do, but I guess I was just feeling really desperate."

"I need you to promise me that you won't abandon her again. Her little heart can't take it. She's your daughter, and she really had a lot of problems these last few years because you weren't around. She needs her father, and I'm begging you not to disappear on her again."

"I promise. You know, I thought I was coming here because I wanted to get a bone marrow match, but as soon as I saw her I realized that if I died, I wanted to be at peace with the relationship I had with her. I felt a lot of regret. We've had a hard road, and that has been my fault. But I promise that I will never leave her again. It was the worst mistake of my life."

She nodded. "You missed out on a lot of great things, Brandon. But there are a lot of wonderful memories to be made in the future, and if I can do my part to give the both of you that opportunity, then I consider it an honor."

He reached over and squeezed her hand. "You don't know how much this means to me, and I certainly don't deserve it. But, thank you anyway."

Kate never imagined that she would be sitting in this situation, holding Brandon's hand beside his hospital bed and planning on how to save his life.

Six Months Later

Kate and Mia stood behind the table, waiting for their first customer to show up. The Carter's Hollow Summer Festival was the biggest event of the year, and Sweet Charlene's Honey had its very own table at the event. They couldn't wait to get their first sale.

"Any takers yet?" Darrell asked. He'd insisted on being a part of the big day after getting the first jar of honey from Kate's hives. He told her it was the best honey he'd ever had, although Kate thought he might be partial. "You know, some say beekeeping is the second oldest profession."

"Oh really?" Mia said, trying to feign interest. Darrell was full of useless information.

"Hey, Darrell, do you mind getting me and Mia some lemonade? They have the best stand down there at the end of the road."

Darrell nodded his head. "Sure! I might even get

me one of those corndogs I saw earlier..." he said as he continued walking. Darrell didn't seem to care if anyone was actually listening to him. He just liked to talk.

"Thank you. I love him to death, but it's like sitting next to an encyclopedia that's just blurting out random information," Mia said, laughing.

"Am I your first customer?" They looked up to see their father, Jack, standing there with Sylvia.

"Oh my goodness! I didn't know you guys were coming to the festival. I'm so happy to see you! It's been months." Kate walked around the table and hugged them both.

"I know, I know. Between having my procedure and trying to do my cardiac rehab, my calendar has been full. But they released me last week, and I'm good as new!" Jack rubbed his chest.

"Well, I wouldn't say good as new. You're still an old geezer in my eyes," Sylvia said, smiling up at him.

"Seriously, what did the doctor say about your progress so far?"

"He's really happy. My arrhythmia is gone, and my heart function improved ten percent during rehab. They are switching me to a plant based diet, which is not something I ever thought I'd do. You know how I love hamburgers."

"But he's doing it because he wants to live a long life with his daughters and beautiful wife," Sylvia said, poking him in the side.

Kate was very happy to see them getting along so well. They had really had a rough patch when her dad first got diagnosed, but when he finally gave in and opted for the ablation, everything turned around. They seemed closer than ever.

"So, how much is this Sweet Charlene's Honey?" Jack asked.

"For you, it's free," Mia said, handing him a jar.

"I guess it pays to know people in high places," he joked.

"Well, I guess we're going to do a little walking around. Jack promised that I could buy some wonderful candles I smelled on the way over to your table."

"I don't remember promising anything…"

"We'll see you girls later," Sylvia said, smiling as she pushed Jack out into the pathway.

"I can't believe he's here. I'm so glad he's doing so well," Mia said.

"How is business?" Cooper asked as he walked up behind Kate and slid his arms around her waist. She looked up at him.

"Well, we haven't sold a thing so far, so business is actually pretty slow."

"The way I see it, you have to get people interested in your product. Why don't we put out some samples?"

"That's a good idea. Mia, do you still have those little plastic cups. Maybe we could use those?"

"I'd be glad to walk around and stir up some business," Cooper said.

"My hero," Kate said, smiling. Mia handed him a jar of the honey and a few of the cups.

"Anything for my *honey*," Cooper said, laughing. "Get it? Honey?"

Kate and Mia both rolled their eyes. "Get to work, funny guy."

As they continued standing behind the table, Kate wondered if her honey business had been a good idea or not. Everyone just kept walking past the table, and she was starting to second-guess things when an older woman walked up, a big smile on her face.

"Hi. Welcome to Sweet Charlene's Honey. Would you like a jar?"

"Oh, yes, please. Charlene was one of my dearest friends back in school."

"Really?"

"Yes. We served on student council together back in high school. I'd like to buy three jars, please. There's nothing better than honey on a nice warm buttermilk biscuit with a little bit of extra butter added."

Kate smiled. She would never totally understand southern cooking, but it was definitely the epitome of comfort food.

She bagged up the three jars of honey and took the woman's debit card, swiping it across the little device that she had on her cell phone. She asked the woman if she could take her picture since she was her first customer, and she happily obliged.

After she walked away, Mia and Kate had a private little celebration. "I guess we are truly in the honey business now, aren't we?" Mia said.

"I guess we are. Who knew this is where we would be this time last year? Sisters, boyfriends, Dad… And now honey?" Kate said.

"I guess you never really know where life is going to take you."

A few minutes later, Evie sped past the table on a scooter. Following behind her were Abigail and Elijah, her brother and sister. Brandon and his wife had opted to move to Atlanta shortly after his bone marrow transplant. They were impressed with the hospitals, and Brandon wanted to be closer to Evie.

Many weekends, they would come up to Carter's Hollow and spend time with her, letting the kids get to know each other and sometimes even staying at the B&B. Kate and Kara couldn't have been any different, and she wasn't really all that fond of the woman, but she and Brandon had mended fences enough to be good co-parents to Evie.

"Slow down on that thing!" Kate said, waving her hand at Evie as she flew by. Evie groaned and kept going, her siblings following after her like ducklings.

She was very happy that Brandon was considered to be in remission, although he would have to take anti-rejection drugs for the rest of his life. He still had to be careful and go to his doctor appointments to make sure that things were still going well. From what she could tell he was finally getting back on his feet.

Kara, although not her favorite person, had thanked Kate on multiple occasions. Of course, Evie had also thanked her mother time and again for what she had done. But to Kate, there had been no other choice. You help people, even when it's someone you may not understand or like.

Mia had told her that she got that from their mother, and Kate was starting to believe that genetics were a strong factor in her life.

"Where's Travis?"

"He's down at his table. After working on that book, he is in high demand now. I'm surprised he even has time to sell his photographs at an event like this. He's been fielding offers from all over the world."

"How do you feel about that? I know you don't want to be away from each other very much," Kate said, rearranging the jars of honey for the twentieth time that day.

"He's only working on projects that might take him away for a day or two, but anything longer he's pretty much turning down. Although, he did get one offer in the Caribbean, and we're thinking about making a trip out of it. I hope you can watch the B&B if we do that?"

Kate laughed. "I think I can help you out with that. You deserve to see the world, sis. Mom would understand if you left the B&B sometimes."

"I know, I know."

As Kate stood back and looked around at the festival, she could see all of the different people that she loved. Evie was zipping around in the parking lot with her two adoring siblings behind her. Cooper was walking up and down the pathway, trying to convince people to have a bite of honey. Her dad and Sylvia were smelling candles at a table off in the distance. And of course, her sister was standing right next to her, always her sidekick and best friend.

There was nothing that Kate could imagine that would be better than this. No, this life was getting sweeter all the time.

***

Visit www.RachelHannaAuthor.com to see a list of Rachel's book including the next one in this series!

Made in the USA
Monee, IL
20 March 2022